T0086326

A Reshaped View

A Reshaped View

GABRIELLE F. CULMER

A RESHAPED VIEW

iUniverse books may be ordered through booksellers or by contacting:

iUniverse
1663 Liberty Drive
Bloomington, IN 47403
www.iuniverse.com
844-349-9409

ISBN: 978-1-6632-4918-0 (sc)
ISBN: 978-1-6632-4917-3 (e)

Library of Congress Control Number: 2023909133

Print information available on the last page.

iUniverse rev. date: 05/12/2023

1 | Back to Normal

Kascey looked onto brilliant scenery on a vibrant autumn day. Her view through the large bay windows was from the penthouse floor of a manor hotel situated in the heart of Mayfair within driving distance to the shows. The room was luxurious with grey carpeting, ornate walls, delicate moulding, high ceilings with full lighting, and a settee and table where she had set sustainable silk, soft material, and her planners. It was her first show in the new normal since starting Kascey Couture. She had become a style icon, and the name encompassed all her dreams and aspirations. It was the brainchild of the culmination of her life's work, which had taken her from her early years in her parents' fabric manufacturing company in Canada, to her studies in the Parisian fashion district, to being the understudy and associate to a famous Latin American designer in New York. Now she was a married woman with her own line, her staff, and models for international shows.

Her best friend and internationally acclaimed model Moda was in the entourage and had been specifically picked for her ensemble. Moda would be the face of her creations. Soft palettes of creams, pinks, and baby blues would soften the effects of the change of normality. A socially distanced and independent message of relaxation and patience with a universal Internet audience would communicate hope to the world. The way that the sustainable fabric moved and draped her figure was incentive to the public to keep fit and survive. Kascey knew what it had been like and was grateful. She had found a newly formed love with and faith in Gradey. She relished the quiet walks through parks with Gradey, early mornings spent watching the sunrise and taking in the smell of pancakes, and late nights with fairy lights and homemade dinners on the terrace. There were decisions to use whatever was in the pantry and on order. She savoured watching the dark skyline from across the Hudson with few lights as the city slept during the pandemic.

Now there was a sense of rebirth. Her recollection of having to leave the office in midtown late in the evening with its quiet and solitude remained. The city had a remoteness to life and uncertainty of revival. The antithetical reaction to a crisp and clear spring day. The days of isolation seemed over as she and Gradey isolated in their new river view apartment in downtown Manhattan. She cringed at the thought of a high floor now, considering that in the case of a power surge, they would be stuck. She reminisced of the outdoors and the country. They had even considered moving. They had overcome the new normal.

Now she was Kascey Chisol after nine months of marriage to Gradey, who was the man of her dreams and who had flown the earth to be with her. Memories of their former lifestyle of romantic dinners in the Flatiron District, the bustle of Midtown, the mystique of Paris, and the romance of Venice and Monaco were distant memories. Her show items would represent what life now meant to her: the toned-down mood, the practicality of an essential job, the safety and security of one's home and sofa—more than the bustling lifestyle and the glamour of the streets of New York. But she reminisced on the smaller things in life: the holidays and Thanksgivings; her family, and family visits to the cape; barbecues of shellfish and late nights on the beach and the coastal village. Her maturity had now placed her on her own two feet and ready to display her hard work to New York, Paris, and Milan.

She was getting used to the new normal and the new sense of style that had overcome the wave of the pandemic. Her materials were flowing, and her style relaxed. She had designed a few couture gowns for the adventurous, but the stages had changed, and so had she. Those gowns were soft and flowing. Her gusto was revived, but not long ago it had been deflated. In the past, she had relied on family to get through it, and she recollected the extraordinary circumstances that they all had faced. She thought that at one point it could all fold, but she was grateful for the financial support. It was the one thing that she could rely on as long as it was possible with the notion that others were not as lucky.

Fortunately, her family and friends also survived virtually, but she missed some along the way. It seemed that luck had been distributed sparingly, and she reserved prayers for those who were suffering. There was a fear that had been associated with it all which inspired the desire to have soft shades to smooth it over—nothing too dreary, only simple enough to be comforting. Her ensemble had taken on a new shape from fitted to flowing, from decorated too socially distanced. She was determined that Kascey Couture would survive for the greater good.

It was like returning to the beginning. She had navigated through the pandemic, keeping up with the markets along with the sewing machine in her guest room and packaging merchandise in her living room and going totally online with the suppliers. She had overcome the hassle and the anxiety of shipping and packaging. She looked forward to the allure of online sales as incentive. Most of all, her supportive husband developed his whole business online amidst a failing market which was out of his control, with the pandemic to blame.

She knew that her former boss, Vasquez Lake, would be on the virtual show route, and she could use his advice more than ever. The pandemic had had a harsh effect on his business. Being stationed in Westchester with Daphne and the children brought comfort. However, there was less need for couture, and he had just fully turned his business online. Starting the shows again in the socially distanced world was challenging; however, he himself was a survivor, having built an empire as a second-generation American from South America. This show would exhibit his ability to survive with an emphasis on the coming spring as being the revival and rejuvenation that the world needed to enlighten moods with bright yellows and peach wraps for those on casual outings, as sparse as they might be. It would take a new turn with outdoor walks and open-air venues. He was faced with the issues regarding the privacy of the Internet and sensitive material regarding his work as he navigated the show from the comfort of his cosy fireplace and rustically decorated living room in the States. After the last theft of a dress almost two years ago, he was cautious about using the Internet and grateful to not be dealing with the risk.

Kascey's mobile rang.

"Hi, it's me," a female voice stated. "Just checking in. I have done all the protocol and will get to the venue in half an hour."

"Great, hair and makeup should be there. I will leave now. Good luck, Moda," she replied familiarly.

"Thank you. Looking forward to it and thank you for the opportunity. It sure beats being dressed up in a visual box from my living room."

"I know. Let's hope things do not get worse. I am on my way now. No worries, you were always meant to be the face of my brand."

"Perfect, and I feel really privileged. Ciao."

"Ciao." On that note, she gathered her bag and tried to collect herself. It felt euphoric but strange to be getting out there again as if nothing had happened. It was more noticeable in Europe, but New York still had ground to cover. However, she and Gradey could hear the activity below from their terrace. There was excitement on the pavements with restaurants having remote openings. Sometimes they did not have the ability to order, as it was too risky. In consequence, she had shed a few pounds just improvising with what was already in the fridge and rationing. She felt reassured, as though they were saving someone's life just by making the decision to stay in or avoid the area. It was intriguing how much she thought of others more, offering food donations and free or bargain items to loyal customers. She also thought of friends and family members who were less fortunate and needed donations, as small as they could be.

~~~~~~~~~~~~

Kascey's car pulled up to the show's venue. There were still a few more hours, and she wanted it to be perfect. She marvelled at the signage and her name on the boards and tickets. First she checked the wardrobe to see if it all had arrived. She had recalled the last time that the most premier gown of Vasquez's show had gone missing between the airport in New York and the hotel in Paris. It was still a mystery as to how it ended up replicated a few weeks later. The lesson always hung over her head, especially when she travelled.

She had her temperature checked and was tested before entering. The protocols were intense for the show. Even the lighting seemed softer, or perhaps it was her imagination. She recognized a few of her entourage in hair and makeup, which was being applied by conscientious stylists. She was masked and wearing cotton gloves. The show would take place on the rooftop, where the models would be left to the contrast of the soft clothing in natural lighting and the breath of fresh air.

She recognized Moda's lengthy build and cardigan as she was prepared for the show. Kascey took over a few items to check the compatibility of the material's shades with the makeup.

"Hey," she gasped beneath her mask as she slightly turned to Kascey.

"It's perfect," encouraged Kascey as she observed the hairstyle.

"Great." She gleamed back with smiling eyes, unable to communicate otherwise over the sound of the dryers.

Kascey was struck with a bit of yearning. She thought of happier times, in which the atmosphere was electric and the audience abundant times when Vasquez was hurtling through and she would follow him with the dresses as she decided who wore what. There was loud music and champagne with vivacious and grandiose gesturing. Gone were those days, and probably it was a good thing that Vasquez was missing it, as she did not know how he would have coped without it all.

Kascey looked around to find a few more models from her entourage and checked on them. It was soon time to get upstairs, where there were a few planners, organizers, and camera operators. There would be a universal airing, and from one spot her work would be on the global stage.

The models filed out in her lounge pastels, displaying her work with the ease and confidence they had been trained to display. She was in awe, with the natural sunlight shining on the smooth fabric and on loose hairstyles, as well as the shimmery and basic make-up, which gave a sun-kissed look. The ending showed Moda in a silk Grecian-draped gown in pastel pink. It was shimmery and sat on her frame statuesquely. Her high cheekbones and sharp features behind a mask contrasted the movement of the gown to provide a perfect pairing.

Her husband, Gradey, who was present and attended online, texted her from their skyline apartment in Manhattan. "Beautiful. It all looks great. I knew that you could do it. One down and three more to go!" Kascey felt assured by his words of encouragement. He was always seemed to be there at the right moment.

"Thanks dear, miss you loads and loads."

"See you in a few days. XO"

"XO"

Kascey applauded them as she rose to take her walk with them. Although there was no large crowd to applaud, she still felt invigorated and relieved by it all. Her petite brunette frame countered the tall models around her and almost provided her with the accentuation she needed to stand out among them. Even in high heels, she still was not equal in height to Moda, to which she was accustomed. She never was affected by this and had even had Moda stand in her wedding.

"Thanks, ladies, and here is to Paris and Milan. Now, see you back at the suite for some refreshments." It was a tradition set by her old boss, Vasquez, which she continued, albeit in a very distanced way this year.

Kascey was relieved by the success of the show. She could

not believe her luck as to her survival and ability to pull it all off in a different city. She had good advice and financial planning and knew that there was a strength behind her motivation—Gradey.

~~~~~~

Gradey Chisol was the love of her life. He was her soul mate, who had wooed her and taken her on the most beautiful trips before the pandemic. His face at their wedding next to the sunset on the beach had said it all. To him, he was looking at the most beautiful woman in the world, and she had found the man that she had wanted all her life. She knew that he was the one from the night that they met. She recalled it well. It was at a party, and his sister Lucy had introduced them. His sister was the buyer at Marleys NY, and Kascey had just moved to the city from Paris. Gradey had impressed her the whole night. It felt as if she had talked to him for ages, and they had so much in common. She'd had vacations in Bimini, and he'd had vacations in St. Barts. She had trained in Paris, and he had trained in Switzerland, and the similarities were discovered over the course of the evening.

In New York, Gradey checked the time, and it was almost 2.00 p.m. Kascey was on British time and almost finished with her show. He imagined the stress that she was under with the new protocols and the first time that she had been away in almost a year. He imagined that she was still in the apartment, sketching her designs or on the computer. He awaited his lunch order from the Mexican restaurant down the block. It would be evenings of enchiladas for the week until she returned. His parents were in Maine, riding out the pandemic safely, and his sister was in Connecticut with her new beau, Nate. His colleagues from the cape had left and were still working from home.

He sat at his desk and imagined his office and the thought that it would soon return to normal. The large room overlooked the skyline. He recalled the energy that encircled the room when he walked in with his colleagues and staff perched on the desks in front of their computers inside their fishbowl-type offices. He got back to work; the nostalgia would only defeat his purposes, and now they were planning a takeover for a casualty from the pandemic. Salvaging companies had become the norm with bankruptcies on the rise. It saddened him that it had all come to this.

"What is happening?" he asked Claude.

"Tirogam is going under and looking for a bailout."

"What is the value?" he asked excitedly.

"About twenty-five per share."

"Probably will be worth nothing in a few days."

"Try to see if they will take fifteen per share and a few bonds?"

"I don't know."

"It's all crumbling. Just see. We are running low on equity, and another offer might come in to consider. Sorry, friend; it is the best that we can do," he replied sympathetically.

Venture capitalism was not easy during these times and could be severe. He found it difficult living his dream. He had everything that he wanted, and he had been left to work at home, with his wife around the world and the funds dwindling. He needed an infusion, and he securely and almost childishly thought that he need not look further than the proverbial Bank of Mom and Dad. He planned to offer them shares in the company for the loan. He would be lucky to get $10 million, although $25 million was needed to relieve all the companies.

Luckily, Kascey had downsized to reduce operational costs. She had fewer staff and had moved her operations to their sofa in the living room. Her business rent had been suspended, as was most of her contingency until the end of the month. Paying for the show and the models came out of capital saved from the initial startup investment when she opened. She was luckier than many who had their businesses shuttered. Had she not moved when she did, she would have been out of a job. She was relieved that hindsight was golden and 20/20 vision and even luckier when it moves your way.

―――――――

Kascey had a few canapés and beverages brought to the suite. There were only a few ladies present, as they had to remain in the same bubble of a small group. The trip, which was part of the production of the show, had been carefully planned. The small number of ladies sat and chatted about the independence and motivation of the day while they watched the clips from the show as it was streamed online. The fall season was vibrant in Europe before the arrival of the second wave.

"That looks marvellous," Kascey exclaimed in awe.

"I see that. Wonderful dress," replied Moda.

"Humility was never a strong point," joked Chantelle.

"I know, but thanks. You wear it well," answered Kascey.

"Thanks. All the items draped so well."

"Yes. I loved the collection," responded Chantelle.

"I think that it is perfect for the spring," Mirielle responded.

Mirielle was new to the scene, and it was her first show. She had debuted with effortless charm and beginners' luck with an interesting look. She was raised in New Haven and was built very slim, but tall enough to carry the designs. She was a comparable addition to the entourage, as her chiselled features were compatible with those of Moda, who remained the centre of attention.

Kascey checked her laptop and noticed that it had been on for most of the day. She was still connected to the server and had not signed out of her company's accounts. A few emails had returned, and she remembered that she had not sent them. A surge of anxiety went through her as she flicked through her screen pages. The situation did not automatically look right.

"Odd," she murmured. "I thought that I left this off and had signed out." She noticed that the emails that had returned had been sent to fake addresses. "Oh no," she gasped. "I have been hacked." She knew instinctively and panicked as she ran the safety scan on the system and found malware. She called her technician back in New York, who had to remotely test her system's server.

"Sorry, ladies. I have to attend to this," she said with a hollowed and frantic heart.

They answered considerately in the affirmative, sensing her distress.

"*Oh no,*" she murmured. "They have come for the designs and as it appears sophisticatedly online." She gasped and thought of ways to protect the rest of the line, but it was too late. The new line would be on the fake market before day's end. There would be online knock-offs of her originals. She was fearful of what was to come. She spoke to the technician frankly.

"Val, I think that I have been hacked or something!" she said.

"Sorry about that, and let me look," he replied in disbelief. "There are some international rogues working. Can you please send me the returned emails, and I will investigate from this end?"

"Sure. Do you think that they got much?" she inquired.

"That all depends on what you have stored in the cloud and perhaps on the PC."

"Well, no bank accounts, but my work and contacts," she confessed.

"Okay. I am not sure what they might have been after on this. Send me what you think is suspicious, and do not open anything. Also, if you have the server ID of the hotel, I can check with them."

"Right, will do. I hope that this is not serious."

"Well, that is what we are trying to determine. Have you clicked on any strange links recently or received any phishing emails over the last few days?" he asked.

"I will have to check. I don't think so," she answered cautiously. The response made him cringe. She had probably been targeted. "What would they be after?" she continued.

"I am not sure right now. Leave it with me, and I will have a progress report in a few hours," he reassured her.

"Thanks. I just want to say that I experienced something before with my old boss Vasquez, and someone stole the designs between airports."

"Thanks for that information, and I will bear that in mind; but I really do not know if there is a connection, as this is a different type of attack."

She hung up, despondent, with the same eerie feeling from the last time almost two years ago in Paris. Gradey had arrived, and they had discovered that the main encore dress had been nicked. This time she was without her emotional rock. She had to call him.

"Look. It seems as though something horrible has happened on my computer," she confessed to the group. "Excuse me while I call Gradey. I will go in the other room," she said as she abruptly left again.

"Sure, and take as much time as you need. Let us know if you need anything," Moda replied, sounding concerned. and not having seen her this agitated in a long time.

"I will. Just give me a second to address this issue." She walked to the bedroom, closed the door, and dialled him as soon as she could.

"Hey. How did the rest go? From what I saw it looked terrific," he said optimistically.

"Thanks, and it went well. Did you see it all?"

"Yes. I saw the link, and then Claude called. It all looked good from here. I saw you after on the catwalk. Now, tell me, what is it? You sound stressed." He grew more concerned.

"Everything. I am stuck here, and we fly to Paris tomorrow.."

"Well that is not too bad. You are still able to fly while some of us can't."

"All of that aside, someone has hacked into my account, and I have this feeling that they were after the designs. Nothing else was affected, and I have no bank accounts active on that computer."

"Oh dear, are you sure? I am so sorry. Did you call Tech?"

"Yes, and Val is working on it. But my mind is so distracted from the show."

"Do not worry. It is now important to concentrate and get your authentic style out first. They cannot concoct an entire dress line in a day. Try to get your work out there and put your stamp on it. The authorities will deal with this once it is reported. Val will have to report the fraud. On the other hand, this could just be a mountain made out of a mole hill. Now take it easy; I am here, and I will see you in a few days. Remember: someone is working on it. I will call Val now so that we can get this thing over with."

"Lovely," she said as she breathed a sigh of relief. "You always know how to cheer me up. Love you."

"Love you too. Have a great evening, and try to keep your

mind off it. Did you change your passwords? I am sure you will."

"Yes, dear. I shall."

"Call me if you need me, and talk to you later," he reassured her.

"Bye." She ended the call and opened her computer to initiate the changes. It felt like déjà vu. She hated the idea that she was to go to Paris with this on her mind like the last time that she was there with Vasquez Lake. She missed her old boss during times like these. It had been such a shock when it happened. She pushed aside the thought that there was a connection.

"Sorry to put a damper on everything, ladies," she apologized. "The show must go on. Now we have to wrap up early and get ready for the flight tomorrow."

"Hear, hear," they cheered, happy that she was back after her inspiring Gradey pep talk.

2 | Dim Lights

Gradey wanted to assist Kascey and was on the line sorting out the hacking issue. It was his chivalric instinct when it came to the woman of his dreams. He sat on the phone with Val to try to work it out for her, as he could detect her distress thousands of miles away.

"Fine, Val, try to figure out where they might have placed the missing files," he requested.

"Will do. I can't believe that she was targeted," he said in disbelief. "I can see where the design files were accessed during the show. However, she was at the venue. So it was not her. They must have hacked in the system."

"Have there been any demands?" Gradey asked, sounding alarmed.

"Nothing yet. I presume it was about the files and not for any ransom. We are dealing with a unique hacker with what could be a different intention," Val replied.

"Perhaps. It might be a different outcome. In any event, it has to be reported. Have you alerted her?"

"Not yet. It is very late. I will send an email when she

awakes. I have given her a list of precautions to take and have locked the account to avoid further intrusions," Val confirmed.

"Great, and thanks for your hard work. Let me know if there is anything that I can do for you if you cannot reach her. I promised her that I would look into it."

"Sure thing, and not a problem. I will keep you posted once we figure out who it might be. There are a number of fake merchandise scammers out there, and I will keep an eye out to see if there are any similar designs and attire being launched."

"Thanks, and send me a list of which websites to check, as she is inundated."

"Right, will do. I will keep you posted," answered Val.

"Thanks." Gradey hung up. He had no idea how to break the news to her or to solve this for her before she returned.

Kascey had worked so hard on this collection, and to have it swiped from beneath her was horrifying. Gradey tried to tell himself that it was not personal. He had to go into a more reactive mode to what might occur. He had to determine whether there was a way to save this collection from entering the fake market and what was the price to pay. He had to also think about saving his own business. The stress built as he thought of everything at the same time.

Gradey reflected upon the view of the Hudson. He missed the lights of the boats mooring on the river's edge and the vast skyline from his office. He still wanted to be further downtown, and the move was to be closer to Kascey's business. He took the days without her in stride. He was upon the last part of the day, whereas she was fast asleep. She had been with him through so much: the Jacob Commerciale investigation regarding the IPO, the travels, the business startup, and now this—a pandemic the likes of which had not been seen in one hundred years. He was not sure how they would have survived it had it been one hundred years ago. Then the war broke out and the markets sank. He definitely would not have been able to survive that. It was what he lived for. All these issues entered his mind.

The bell rang. It was DoorDash with an order from Pinelli's, their favourite Italian restaurant. At least that had survived of what had been between them. It was now about the new memories and their favourite haunts around the city, which were also in survival mode and were about to reopen fully.

He had those memories with Kas, Caleb, and Lucy on the cape, which had subsided now. He yearned for the cape and what they had missed this last Labor Day and the many they had spent before then: the walks along the shore, the late nights with friends on the veranda, family meals, and taking the boat along the sound. He thought of Jane, the housekeeper who cooked the wonderful meals, and how she was ensconced and shielding in the small town. His parents were in Maine, and Luce and Nate in Connecticut. There was little correspondence with his secretary Norma, as well as his old colleague Germaine, who was now in Europe.

He heard the buzzer again; the food had arrived. He looked at the terrace, which was now vacant. It had been a refuge where they would dine, laugh, and dance while the world was still turning in a quieter way, far away from the unrest. He yearned for her laughter.

He opened the glass door of the terrace. There was a crisp autumn breeze to complement his crisp, cool beer. A knock was heard, and he went to the front door to collect his meal.

He had ordered her favourite and stored it in case she appeared. It would be another estimated three days before he saw her. He could hear the echo of her promise to get on the flight just after the show from Milan and to reach their apartment by evening after passing through the time zones back to where she belonged. He had no idea how he had become so codependent. This was something that she had done all the time when they met and had now got harder. He could not face the possibility of losing her and wanted her back soon.

Paris had revived a little since the pandemic. The thought of those starry nights in the crisp cool and the shop lights still remained. However, there was now social distancing, with masks being worn everywhere, and people took advantage of outdoor activities as long as they would last. The venue was outdoors, and again everyone was tested. It was a challenge to get the merchandise to the models, as there was a strict code of her access to them. The measures would be only for a short while, and she was confident with the stringent rules due to the pandemic. There would also be less risk of something else going wrong. Kascey accepted the risk to get her work out at a time when the supply would be lower as a result of the production reduction in the industry. It was her opportune moment, and she would attempt to be as safe as possible.

Val had sent her the emails. She had the feeling that something had gone horribly wrong and that her designs had been stolen and would be used on the fake market. Her solution was to change them and shift the colours to mauves and silvers and some of the lounge wear to her signature asymmetrical off-the-shoulder vibe. There was a recycled material fit with the concept of sustainability, whereas her gowns would be fitted. The Grecian-draped gown was still a hit; however, there would be varieties that the thieves would not be able to duplicate in time.

She wanted to talk to Vasquez, who had become a fabulous mentor. She knew that to relay her experience to him would be like déjà vu.

She gave him a call. "How is it all going, Kascey?" he asked with trepidation.

"It could be better. I am calling to wish you luck. I know that this is your stomping ground."

"Yes it is. We are all ready, and I cannot wait to watch it from here in Westchester. I must say that the photos look phenomenal."

"Well, the venue is superb. The perfect weather for the entourage to be outdoors amongst the picturesque gardens of the chateau. I will drive out there later. They have gone ahead," she said.

"Great. Please tell them hello for me and good luck!"

"I will, and I am sure that you have spoken to Moda and Talia."

"Yes I have, and they are ready for my show this evening. You go first. Age before beauty," he responded sheepishly.

"That is so funny. You always had a way of making me laugh. On a sourer note, we've been hacked and my designer files have been accessed."

"That is terrible. What are you going to do?" he asked apprehensively.

"I have no idea. Perhaps change my styles so that I will be unique and get my designs out first, I guess. Have an injunction granted ... a report on them is all in the works."

"Sorry to hear that. It reminds me of that time in Paris. Certain people never give up and can want something for nothing. It is so intrusive and deceptive. What a horrible thing to happen."

She knew that he sympathized with her and remembered her prior experience, which was not on such a grand scale. It was the first time she had been targeted.

"Thank you for your concern dear. I am sure that this too will pass," she responded hopefully.

"It will pass, and good luck today. I will be watching. Remember to enjoy your opportunity. I am immensely proud of you."

"Thank you. You also have a successful day. I can't wait to see the line," she replied appreciatively.

She felt some relief as they disconnected. There was so much now to figure out. She had a feeling that it could have been competitors or maybe a targeted hack. There was nothing random about the motive. The motive was to get the designs, and it was done to her, and now she had to deal with it. She heard the buzzer; and it was her driver to the show. There was the pandemic to deal with, and now there was also the issue of starting a new line in the middle of the presentation.

Val had reported the IP address and cyber information to Interpol. He was apprehensive about any luck right away. They would soon reveal their identities to commit the next stage of their deceit. In the meantime, Kascey drove to the outskirts of Paris to the chateau, where there were vans and attendants waiting. She waved her security card and entered the area for the hosts. The models were preparing for their show while Kascey had her hair styled for her walk. The outdoors gave an air of relaxation; however, the venue was more grandiose against the large backdrop and would increase the visibility of the clothes in the natural breeze and the interest of the world viewers. The atmosphere was dynamic and full of vitality as the show kicked off. The models professionally glided along the catwalk in their shimmering evening outfits and loungewear. They were styled to high fashion and motivated by their aspirations of being on the world's stage. It was broadcast to a wider audience than before the pandemic. The way to take advantage of the shift was to be in the right place at the right time. This had kicked off successfully, and her life was finally coming together. She was inspired by her experience and had wondered what the last few months were about, but now her challenging work had been rewarded.

"Well done," she congratulated the models from two metres away as they all filed out on stage again. She also walked in file behind them as the denouement to the evening occurred. There was a murmured applause as they left the stage. It was to be expected from the socially distantly spread audience, who were a handful of privileged industry members. It was the perfect end to a Paris night.

The sun had dimly set in a fresh autumnal evening and a slight breeze had set in as they entered their hotel overlooking the plaza exhausted from the day.

"One down and one more to go," Kascey exclaimed as they each retired to their rooms.

The models thanked Kascey before they finally got their much needed rest and room service.

Kascey entered her suite, which had been turned down, and flopped on the settee. She pulled out her phone and called her husband.

"How is it?" she asked.

"How is what? New York?" Gradey asked.

"Yes. What is it like?" She was inquisitive, as she missed it.

He looked through the window, "A bit breezy today from what I can tell. Sunny and bright. About sixty degrees."

"Fine. What are you up to?" she inquired, satisfied.

"Just going over some statistics for the buyout. Nothing special. I always have time for you. What is happening?"

"I guess you missed the show?"

"No. I saw some of it, dear. It looked great. I will have to watch it a bit later. This project is the worst. Dealing with a tech company affected by the pandemic, and there is potential, but I have to produce the money fast."

"I see. Sorry to hear that. I hope it all goes well. I am famished and have to order something. Miss you," she responded soothingly.

"Miss you too. See you in two days, right?" he inquired.

"Yes. Two days and then we will be together."

"Have they finalised the NY show?"

"Sure. It will be socially distanced, from different venues and online. Just the basic staff. Judee and Syre will be back from furlough."

"Yes, and give you a bit of rest. You must be exhausted," he empathized.

"Very much. Love you, and take care."

"Love you too."

She ordered her dinner from the app: a simple chicken and frites. It was either that or a packed protein shake. *I should have had the salad*, she thought. She was comforted by the notion that she would make up for it tomorrow, however; there was a plane to catch, and she would be eating the best clam vongole. The room service attendant rang her buzzer and left her meal cart by the door. She hastily retrieved it and rolled it in. *A meal for one*, she thought as she looked at the view of the Eiffel Tower and the plaza from her terrace doors.

Her business travels were not recreational, and she derived little enjoyment from the trips. It took her back to the times she had spent with Gradey before the pandemic—the many times that they had strode through the plaza and up the Champs-Élysées, stopping off at the museums or at their favourite bistro, entwined in each other's company. These journeys had mostly taken place in spring or fall, the most recent last year. How strange that a year could change so quickly—so many lives lost, and so many people in pain from it all. Europe had suffered and was springing back as it did after the Second World War, but the future could still be uncertain. There was a recession, and times were hard, but the economic forecast was still due to make a positive turn.

She ate the meal with a tinge of guilt and lined up the clothing for tomorrow. She was still faced with the notion that her lines could be online at any minute. She tried to be a little more creative and pulled out her mini sewing machine. "No one is making a fool out of me," she said to herself.

⸻

Gradey had something special planned for her return. He would set up the terrace in a Parisian theme and order from the bistro on the corner: her favourite dessert, wine, salads, and entrée. And, of course, there would be music. He missed being with her, and it would be a surprise.

He picked up the phone to do some business of a family nature.

"Hey Dad. How are you?" he asked, upbeat.

"Just fine, son. How are you holding up?" Damian asked with a sense that something was the matter.

"Great. Things are good. Waiting for the city to fully open. Kas is still away. I miss the cape though," he blurted out.

"Yes, we missed the cape this Labor Day. There will be more times, son. I remember the '68 pandemic. Things will turn around."

"That is good to hear. I need to hear that, as funds are low. I have an opportunity to buy out a few companies, and the capital is lowering. I would need at least ten or so to keep it viable. I am asking for a business loan, Dad."

"I see, son. Now, anything that I can do to help you out. What will be your return on the buyout?" Damian asked, exhibiting his usual business acumen.

"I figure that I can turn it around by the spring at more than ten dollars per share. Right now, I want to buy at fifteen dollars, when it was worth about twenty-five per share," Gradey replied persuasively.

"Sounds like a pretty slim chance," he replied. "But I will trust your judgement if you have faith in the company. I can transfer that amount from my corporation. Let me know how it turns out for you."

"Thanks, Dad. I will be able to pay that back once the shares rise. I won't over anticipate the shares rising higher than predicted for some time."

"Sure thing. Your mother is in the garden. We were going to take the boat out on the lake this weekend, but your aunt Maura has been unwell."

"Really?"

"Yes, and you had better give her a call. She had some pains and had to have some preliminary tests run in Boston."

"Oh dear. I had better call her. Is it serious?"

"Sounds so. Looks like we will need some prayers. Your mother is upset, so try not to mention it to her."

"Okay. I am sorry. Send my best to Mum."

"I will do. Kelly is outside and trying to get her mind off things. We will have to travel down next week to see her."

"I understand. Send her my best. Bye, Dad."

"Bye, son, and I will call Burt to make that transfer."

"Thanks. I appreciate it, as the banks are strict at lending at the moment."

"Fine. We will give you a better rate." He laughed.

Gradey hung up torn. He was worried about his aunt. His perspective had changed. His focus was no longer what was going on in the markets at that instant. It was now something that he had no control over and something that he could not change. He wanted to pray as she had taught him. When he looked back, he realized he had been taught many things, including baking brownies, riding horses, hunting for shells, and living a decent life and accepting what was expected of him. There were so many lessons in life, and he had spent so many Thanksgivings and summers at the cape. This would change so much of life as he knew it. Kas was fast asleep, so he called his sister, Lucinda.

"Luce, what's up?" he asked.

"Not much. I am still off work, and Nate is in the den, buying from their distributors."

"Well I hope all is well regardless."

"Yes. Just having a perfect afternoon in Stamford," she answered wistfully.

"Great. Kas is still off, and I just spoke to Dad."

"Have you? Did he tell you?" she asked concerned.

"You knew?"

"Yes, Mum called and we got the news," she admitted.

"What is wrong with her?"

"They think that it is her kidney."

"Really?" he responded, filled with fear and confusion as to how to handle the news.

"Yes. The problem is that she was holding off going to see someone, and it got worse," she replied, full of commiseration.

"No way," he responded helplessly.

"Yes. We hope she will be fine and was in hospital and is now in a rehab centre."

"What? I can't believe it," he replied, astonished.

"Sorry to break the news. I guess Dad did not want to go through the details."

"This is terrible. Did they say how long it will last?"

"Well, she will need a transplant," she added, choked up.

"This is the worst. When will that happen?" he asked in disbelief.

"I don't know. She has been waiting a while. And then there is compatibility and all that."

"I see," he replied despondently.

"Yes, you should give her a call," she advised.

"I will do. I will call her; I just don't want to say the wrong thing."

"She always loved you. There is no wrong thing, as you are family."

"Fine, and thanks for your words of advice. Take care of yourself, Luce. Talk to you soon."

"Yes. Chat soon. By the way, Mum wants a trip to the cape when this is all over. She wants to have nostalgic times again with Aunt Maura and us all. So heads up so that you can plan ahead."

"Great, and thanks."

He hung up despairingly. He could not believe the turn of events. It was going from lukewarm to stone cold. Everyone was getting a share of trauma regardless of the cause. He felt as if his plate had become full.

On the bright side, he had the funding to continue his deals. He had a lovely wife and a wonderful family. There was a brilliant view and a weekend of romance planned. He had to remember the good times with his aunt and family and the Labor Days on the cape at their holiday home, Silent Manor, as well as Thanksgivings and the holidays. The times that they had would get them through the next chapters. He wanted so much for his family and his business. As a venture capitalist, he had infused so much in the corporation that he presumed equity partnership was on the table once it was all over. It was true the pandemic had slowed things down, but he accepted that this pace was the new normal.

3 | Homeward Bound

Kascey's plane flew over Canada en route to New York. She peered out the window at the familiar scene and wondered how her family members were coping. She had not spoken to Mabel, her mother, since the new ordeal. The plane was eerily empty but for a few passengers in business and Moda, Chantelle, and Mirielle. There were cars waiting to collect them once they landed, and a swift ride along the Midtown tunnel and then downtown would have her home to her beloved in just under an hour.

"Bye ladies, and thank you for your efforts. It was a success," she said to them as they got to the exit of the arrival's terminal.

"Right Kas, and see you in a few weeks at the next show. We will have to catch up soon," answered Moda.

"Thank you for everything. It was a blast," chimed Mirielle.

"I know. Superb. See you at the next fitting," replied Chantelle.

"Have a great evening. See you all," she replied hastily

as she eagerly anticipated finally seeing Gradey after such a successful time with the ladies.

She met the driver, who swooped her luggage into the boot of the black saloon and scooted her to her front door. She elegantly disembarked and moved to the door which was automatically opened and waltzed to the elevator to her apartment. She took in the aroma of the new carpeting in the corridor and nudged the door. It was ajar, and the best aroma circulated throughout the apartment.

"Mmm," she murmured, recognizing the locale of the meal. "Honey, I'm home!" she shouted as she got to the door.

Gradey appeared in a chequered apron over his work shirt, a tea towel slung over his shoulder.

"Hello dear, how was your flight?" he asked as he greeted her with a hug and kiss.

"All better now dear," she answered. "What is that fabulous smell?" She asked with her face mask now pushed below her chin.

"Just a little surprise from your favourite French restaurant."

"Really, all of that just for me?" she asked in amazement.

"Yes. Anything for you, dear," he replied.

"Marvellous. Gosh, let me get in and have a seat," she replied as she was still in the door's foyer. "Look at all this ambiance. You really made an effort," she said, looking impressed.

"I know. It is a beautiful night in New York. Look at the terrace. There are so many lanterns and tablecloths, and that place setting you always save from Sonoma."

"I know. My favourite set. Thank you," she replied obligingly.

He was proud of his efforts. "Now go and get settled and meet me on the terrace," he suggested.

"I wouldn't miss it for the world." She went to the bedroom, which was a large, cream-infused decorated room with steel furniture frames. "I'm just going to freshen up," she said as she excused herself.

"All right, dear, I will be here." He gathered the french bread and the wine and took them to the balcony. He played some music on the player from France: Cabrel and Goldman, her favourites.

She returned with a sleek and shimmery pink crushed velvet maxi dress, her light brunette tresses slicked back with gel. She wrapped a cream pashmina around her shoulders. She wore a bit of highlighter to have that last hint of summer and to accentuate her striking cheekbones. It was a very natural look.

"You look lovely. You are so beautiful, Kas. Glad to have you home," he said, mesmerized by her appearance.

"Thank you," she said with a sigh of relief. "I have missed you. Now look at all of this. It is so lovely. There is the beautiful setting and the sunset. Look at the city." Then she observed, "It is a bit quiet for a Friday night, though."

"Yes, that is right," he said as he brought the wine. "Here we are, dear. Some wine perhaps?" He poured the Merlot.

"Thanks, I could use some. I avoided it on the flight just to share a glass with you, dear."

"I appreciate it. Here's to you. Cheers!" he raised his glass to hers.

"Cheers," she said as she took a sip. "Lovely," she continued as she savoured the richness of the wine.

"Wait until you see what else I have," he said enticingly.

"I can't wait. What?" she asked, sounding excited.

"What? Well we have bread and brie, salad, frites, ratatouille, chicken fricassee—the whole works. Dessert is crème brûlée and more wine."

"Just like when we were in Paris," she said with an aura of reminiscence.

"Yes, it is just like it. I am sorry that I was not with you, I had so much to sort out. Anyway, we will get to that later."

"Yes, no business talk. Just about us," she confirmed.

"Yes, and *just* about us," he insisted. "It has been almost three years ago that we met, and you have given me the best whirlwind of my life. My world has changed upside down, and we will have been married one year as of New Year's Eve."

"I know. The night we met … it was a party for the buyers and the designers, and I was talking to Lucy."

"That is right, and I came over and said—"

"'Introduce us.' It was a gorgeous evening. I will never forget it. We talked all night."

"I did not want to leave," he replied.

"I did not want to leave either. I should have stayed," she responded longingly.

"Then I called you."

"Yes. You called me and told me—"

"'I know a good Italian place near where you work.' That's right. I had to call," he said.

"You had to call," she said nostalgically.

He poured her more wine nonchalantly.

"Thanks, not too much for me," she cautioned.

"Okay, just tell me when …" he said, humouring her.

"When. You are hilarious."

"I know. Would you like some bread, cheese, salad?"

"Thanks. Sure. I can't believe the aroma and the evening. It's so romantic." She smiled victoriously as he portioned the food out for them.

They laughed and talked over their feast, which was different to what they'd had over the last few months of budgeting. Kascey tried a bit of everything from the buffet that he had set up. By the end of it all, there were dishes stacked and they ate their dessert. She was mindful of the calories and her new dresses, having managed to do a little shopping.

"Gosh. I think that I have put my shape out of synch this last week," she commented as she indulged on a spoonful of crème brûlée. "I have all my new things to try on."

"No, you haven't. I am sure it looks lovely on you no matter what you eat."

She paused to relish the moment. "Thank you dear." She felt reassured. "Oh, I love this song."

"I know; I picked this out for you. Je t'aime."

"Je t'aime," she replied. The atmosphere was mysterious, and they could hear subtle activity below. The sun had hidden, and the terrace was lit with the lanterns and fairy lights.

"Why don't we leave this all for tomorrow. I am sure you are exhausted."

"I am exhausted, but I want to stay up, I have missed you, and this is a wonderful evening."

~~~~~~

The next morning, the sun entered through the cracks of the drapes and across the comforter. She awoke, and there was a breakfast tray lodged on the side of the bed.

"Morning. What's this? This looks great."

"Yes, I just assembled it just for you," he replied. "Morning."

"I love it. Croissants and a rose. Coffee and juice. How sweet."

"Thanks. Bon Appetit!" She delicately tasted the food on the tray and added some fresh jam to the croissant. "Freshly baked. Good."

"Yes. They just brought it. I hope it didn't wake you."

"No. I was still sleeping," she said as she sipped her coffee.

"Wonderful. I have a bit of news regarding my aunt Maura," he started.

"Really? I hope that she is okay."

"Well, she is at a rehabilitation facility in Boston on dialysis."

"Really? Sounds serious."

"Well, sort of. She is awaiting a transplant."

"What? So sorry, I am in shock," she answered.

"Yes. I was too. I have spoken to her, and she is in good spirits. We are hoping for the best, but Mum is very worried."

"I should think so. I am sorry to hear that. I know how much she means to you."

"Yes. She has been a real influence in my family, and we can't do without her. Mum wants a weekend together at the cape when this is all over."

"Certainly. I would look forward to that. Whatever it takes," she replied amenably.

"I knew that you would be comforting. Thank you for being there and being in my life. I just don't know what I would do without you."

"Of course. I will be here ... always," she replied with empathy.

The weekend went quickly, as she was jet-lagged. The scenery was beautiful with the autumn foliage in the distance and the river starting to come to life. Kascey and Gradey enjoyed it whiling away in the living room and watching films and the sunsets at the end of the day. They passed the time strolling along empty streets and window shopping and reminiscing about what used to be and then languishing on the settee across the terrace with the local delivery. It had become a routine to see the day rise and then end together.

"Summer is over dear," she despaired.

"What a summer it has been. Unlike any summer. I so resonate with so much now. I just hope that things do not get worse," he stated.

"I know. Frightening. In a few days, I must prepare for

the virtual show. Can you believe—an online show? I will be behind the scenes."

"You'll be fine," he reassured her.

"I am still worried about my files. Now I have to concoct a new style. I will not let this defeat me."

"I am sure you will not. You have it in you. I have always told you that."

"I have to check with Val. We are expecting a report on Monday."

"Look, whatever the consequences are, we can deal with it," Gradey said. "You are talented, and you can overcome this. You have before. A new security system is in place, and you have the right staff starting again to help you with the new designs. We will just watch out for the fakes to appear."

"You are right. Thank you, darling," she replied, accepting his theory.

"Now, I have so much to sort for the buyout tomorrow. I am going to just check my messages, and I think I will have an early night."

"Me too. I am still jet-lagged," she replied.

The evening became darker earlier, allowing for comfortable slumber, as they also grew cooler and the crisp autumn air set in.

4 | Misty Monday

Kascey held a meeting via Zoom with her staff in Midtown to start the week on the correct footing. For them to be back in the studio was a novelty, and there were social distancing protocols in place. She had cautiously researched the requirements, and after another negative COVID test on arrival, she received legal advice in getting the business started. The tri-state area was experiencing a below-average rate of infection, and she felt more optimistic. They all were eager to start work after a long hiatus. She presented her vision for the next season as her faithful staff conscientiously took notes.

"What I perceive," she stipulated to Judee and Syre, "is that we need to move from the lounge focus to what women need to wear to get back to work and back to what they love—back to the new normal next spring or fall. I think that we should concentrate on the lounge suit. It should still be a quasi-concept to what we have now, but in darker, more professional colours, like bold blue or rich plum. Not too morose so as to put the pandemic behind them, it will be a way to confirm that we have transgressed to the new normal."

"That is impressive, and I completely get the concept, Kascey," answered Judee.

"Great concept," added Syre. "I know that this will be ace for the new season."

"It will look perfect if added with great high boots," continued Kascey. She stopped to check her notes.

"Do you think that we should preview this?" asked Syre.

"Probably if I can get it next week for the show," confirmed Judee.

"Have we got the line-up for that?" asked Kascey. She paused and looked at Judee.

"Yes, I have it right here. I can send it to you," Judee confirmed.

"Thanks. We need to work on that. Will the first venue be at the Garden?"

"Yes, and I know that it will be socially distanced," confirmed Judee. She checked her schedule.

"How many of us can we have?" Kascey asked. "I know I have to be there, and then Moda and Talia and the rest." Kascey demonstrated her strategic planning skills as she set out the schedule.

"Sure. That is how it will work. Everything has to be in place by Thursday," said Judee.

"Gosh. That is no time at all. At least we had a few extra weeks this year to be prepared. Have we confirmed the online guest list?" Kascey asked.

"Yes. We have two hundred guests confirmed online, but that number is changing," said Syre.

"Right. We should confirm that. In the meantime, I will make sure everything is in place. Some of the designs have been changed again. Also, have we heard from Val?"

"Yes, and I can confirm that he is searching for the hackers. He believes that the designs have been compromised. He put out a trace and reported it, so we should get word back on that soon," responded Syre.

"How awful. That is the last thing that we need. It shows how horrible people can be when we are all having a tough time."

"I know and am so sorry that this is part of our lives. I will follow up today," he said.

Kascey prepared herself for the worst. She knew from his tone that it be any day now that her reproduced and reconfigured files and designs would be replicated and duplicated. She was uneasy and tried to dismiss her fears and move on with the planning. She convened the meeting and had a cup of coffee. She needed it. There was a tough week ahead.

Gradey watched the stock's ticker from his study and then got on the phone. He checked to see whether the transfer had occurred. It was imperative that he buy the shares, and this time he knew that there could be a flat fall. The funds had been received.

"Finally. That is good news," he said to his finance manager.

"Great that you got the help."

"Yes, I am so grateful. It is a loan from them. However, my father said that I should not take the whole problems of the world, as things could work themselves out," he responded reassuringly.

"Hope you got a good rate."

"The best rate in town," Gradey said appreciatively.

He had set up the second bedroom as an office. His secretary, Norma, was back virtually from furlough.

"Hi Gradey. It is great to be back. I am just checking today's agenda."

"Norma, glad to have you back. How has it been?"

"It has been trying. Grateful to be back. And how are you?"

"As good as I can be. I am working on a new deal, so we need the reconciliation memo," he responded.

"Coming right up. I just went through the instructions. Glad that it is good news."

"Yes. It is a bit of a gamble, but I believe in this one," he responded confidently.

"Good luck. I will get this right to you," she responded in her efficient manner.

"Thanks, I appreciate it." He had to get used to seeing a familiar face in a box. But he could not complain; at least he had help with the buyout.

He called Damian. "Thanks, Dad. The funds came through."

"That's all right, son."

"Pay you back … I promise."

"I am sure you will. Take your time. As I have said, this is not an overnight ordeal."

"Thanks for those words of advice, and talk again soon. Wait … how is Maura?"

"She looked rather good. She asked about you. She needs some rest and is looking for a donor."

"Sounds a bit more promising."

"A bit more promising, and we will have to see," Damian agreed.

"We will have to see."

Gradey looked at the share price of Tirogam. It had dropped to seventeen dollars per share. It needed an infusion before moving to junk status. He could offer fifteen dollars per share for sure.

He called Claude to get the offer underway. It had to close by the end of the day.

"The funds are in," he said.

"Good news."

"I need to have that agreement signed by lunch," he informed Claude abruptly.

"Right. I will call them and make a proposal," Claude offered.

"Good. Get back to me." Gradey was short and hasty as they moved through his agenda.

He was tense all morning. He kept monitoring the computer and the phone. It was taking a bit long to get responses. He took that as a good sign that something was being done. He received a green-light message from Claude and felt relieved. The deal had been made, and they were now major shareholders of Tirogam Tech. The next step would be the gruelling process to restructure the company and make complex decisions. It was out in Silicon Valley, and it would be exceedingly difficult to correspond personally because of the restrictions. Perhaps it was an advantage to make dealings less personal and get the company back on track with the share price rising again. It was the right time for the industry, and he had suggestions.

"Kas, are you out there?" he asked as he stepped into the living room. The sun had lit the room and was now at afternoon height over the horizon from the terrace. She was entrenched on the sofa with piles of fabric and her portable sewing machine, wearing magnifying lenses, her hair tucked in a chignon.

"Yes, darling, I am here. Have you had lunch?" She peered at him adoringly above her lenses.

"No, thanks. I have been waiting on the deal. It came through, and I am so relieved. Just waiting on a call now."

"Good news and congratulations. There is some spinach filo pastry and quiche in the fridge. No, I did not make it," she confessed.

"All right, thanks," he replied, grinning. "What is that?"

"A new dress, dear. I have the show coming up next week and wanted something different."

"I understand." The air was still tense over the incident. He noticed that she was becoming more accepting of the situation and pressing forward. He moved on from the conversation.

"Dad and Mom are having a weekend at the cape with Maura later in October. She wants us all there together. It is an unusual time to go, but considering the circumstances … What do you think?"

She smiled as she peered above her lenses. "I think that it is a good idea. Tell her we would love to come. It would be perfect to see them all after such a heart-wrenching summer. It will be beautiful with the autumn foliage and the chilly evening walks along the shore."

"Thanks, darling. I knew that you would understand. What do you say that we take a weekend to the Catskills when this is all over?"

"That would be lovely. Hopefully do some apple picking. Do you remember our first time?"

"Yes. It was quite amusing actually."

"It was not," she replied adamantly. "You needed the assistance. I thought that you were going to fall off that tree," she teased.

"Did not."

"Did too," she replied playfully.

"Where's that quiche? I think that I will have some." He walked towards the kitchen.

"In the fridge, dear."

Gradey continued with the motive to invest in the company and held another conference call with Claude.

"I think that we should have a conference with the CEO, Roger, set up tomorrow," he suggested to Claude.

"You are right, and I think that we should also talk to the operations manager and accounts," suggested Claude.

"Great. You do that, and I will get the agenda running. We need to downsize and to produce at the same time to get the revenues flowing at a lower cost. We need the capital gains figures, and we need everything if we are going to make this work."

"Sure thing. I will get right on this."

"And Claude, you can ask Norma to help you, as she returned today."

"Great. We could use our staff again."

"Yes. Such a pity Tirogam may not be able to say the same thing. It is hard enough as it is. We must figure out how to save as much valuable staff as possible. Perhaps a time period to get them back when the company resumes trading at its potential."

"Yes. I think something a bit more humane is in order."

"Right. Thanks, and get back to me with that," he replied ending the discussion.

Gradey needed to think of the state of affairs that was occurring. He wanted to remain positive and not sound like the prophet of doom. He understood that businesses had to take their brunt of the blow to the community. But a line had to be drawn somewhere, or else there would be no viability and it would all be useless in the end. He saw it as using inflating air to build a company from nothing to watch it all crumble again. He had learned his lesson from the last fiasco with Jacob

Commerciale and would not make a mistake with this one. He had a reputation in this town to protect, after all.

~~~~~~~~~~~~~~~~~~~

Kascey had just put down her new gown for the evening. She was creating a glamorous and flowing silk maxi dress. It looked like her good friend Moda's type, and it was her final dress to be worn at the show.

She received a call from Val and knew what it could be, so she dreaded answering it. "Sorry to disturb you," he stated despondently. "I had to call once we have found out the information. There is a new website with what appears to be your designs on it. The culprits have made their move, and the incident has been reported."

"Oh no. I don't believe it. How could they?" she said as her heart sunk.

"I am deeply sorry. It is what we suspected, and of course they are being traced now that this has occurred. I will send you the information, but be careful what details you share when looking this up. Your IP address could be recorded."

"Thank you," she said on cue. "This virtual world has its challenges. I do hope that you find out who has done this and brought me such anxiety and grief when we are all experiencing so much."

"Sure thing. Sorry to be the bearer of bad news," he replied apologetically.

"You are just doing your job; someone has to do it," she said.

"If there is anything else that you need, just call me."

"Thanks," she replied appreciatively.

She hung up disheartened and feeling discouraged, not wanting to continue with her work. Her head started to throb. She called out to her husband, and he came running in to calm her. He cradled her in his arms as she just let it all release from her system: the angst, the grief, the expectation, the loss.

"Shh. Shh. Do not worry. You have more designs. They will get this person. I promise," he replied with indignation.

"I hope so," she said with a sniffle. "This is so frustrating. So deliberate and deceiving. I can never trust using the system. Everything has to change."

"I know. We will sort this out. Luckily, I will be here for the next few weeks until offices open. I will get you through this hon. I swear."

"Thanks. It has been a long day. I will have to take a break and get back to preparing for the show."

"Sure thing. Let's watch something. Some Hulu. Anything you want. And we will order in."

"Sure, that sounds good. Just a salad and some mint tea."

"Whatever you want," he replied as he walked her to the bedroom so she could relax.

He had so much on his plate, yet he had to stick to this one commitment—to have and to hold.

Kas knew that this vulnerable state would not last. She was made of stronger stuff. But to have his attention when she needed it most just for a brief moment meant so much. She would have to pick herself back up on her own two feet in the morning. She had done it before and could do it again. The pandemic had taken more than she could have imagined. As a current survivor, she would rebuild from scratch.

The comforter enveloped her as they lay in the king-size bed, their heads submerged in large pillows, the widescreen TV showing a period drama.

"I appreciate it. This is my favourite and so relaxing."

"I know," he replied, fully aware that he had to get back to the computer. "Take as long as you need to recuperate." He turned on his screen and scrolled through his messages.

"I really need to get back to work. There is so much to do," she confessed.

"Relax. You have staff, and they can handle it. We really need to call in the lawyers now to get these culprits paying some money for what they have done."

"Yes, you are right. They really should pay for their fake enterprise," he replied sarcastically.

"Right. We will call Norsa Shone tomorrow." He was adamant not to let it all get out of control.

"Thanks, and love you."

"Love you too."

After dinner, Gradey got back to work while Kascey had a new infusion of enthusiasm from her well-deserved rest. It revived her soul and her ambitions as she sipped her tea and mentally overcame her obstacles.

Kascey arose to a bright Tuesday. She was determined to start the morning right with exercise before fixing the issues of the previous days. First on the agenda was to call Norsa, the lawyer. She had become familiar with her from the previous ordeal with her former boss and was pleased with the way she had handled it. Norsa would be the first to know whether any of it had the same hallmarks or was connected, as she was very astute.

Norsa had attended an Ivy League law school and had experience in technology, cyber security, and corporate and media law. Her altruistic, traditional, and preppy background never let her step a foot wrong, and she was ahead of the game. She had found a niche in cyber security and was experienced in the field after many years of practice.

Norsa started the virtual conversation full of confidence. "Hello, and I am willing to represent you during the case. I was delighted that you decided to turn to me to assist you with this issue. I'll need you to send me the information from Val, and we can have further discussions then. I can tell you from what you have said that we are looking at a serious offence and you should be entitled to retribution," she convinced her in a northern upper-class accent.

Gratefully Kascey replied, "Thank you for taking the time to talk with me. I am excited that you can represent me. I am really at a loss and had nowhere to really turn."

"Well, rest assured that you have come to the right place. This has become common during the pandemic because of the changes in the security levels at home. No need to worry.

You have all the evidence, and we can really go after them." Kascey could visualize how efficient she could be with Norsa in her patent leather penny loafers and briefcase cornering the culprits, and she was convinced that Norsa was the right person for the job.

After a reasonable discussion, Kascey felt that the call with Norsa was very promising. Norsa was not known as the Detector for nothing. She could detect unconscionability from a distance. She assured Kascey that she would have her associate make enquiries straight away and order an injunction against the culprits. She also explained that the damages would be considerable, along with criminal sanctions.

Kascey breathed a sigh of relief at this advice and felt more inspired to find justice for her pain. She no longer felt vulnerable; rather, she felt empowered by the options that she had. She felt she could now continue with her programme to get the show going.

~~~~~~~~~~

Almost two weeks later, Kascey had remotely set up the sequence of designs. The New York show was socially distanced and had millions of viewers worldwide. She felt the apprehension growing as she dealt with this new scenario which was different than what she had previously experienced. She tried to convince herself that it was the same routine as before in Europe. So much had happened since then, and she felt as though her life had changed. She had added new items to appear more original since her design ideas were swiped.

She enthusiastically applauded the models as they marched confidently along the catwalk in the centre of the virtual world. She watched their steps and how they presented the gowns intricately. She also took her customary walk. It was very strange not to be a full group but to file in individually. It was the new normal, and she had to embrace it.

"Brilliant! I love these designs. They look effortlessly put together, and the sequence so streamlined," noted Chantelle, who was now the coordinator for her former boss, Vasquez Lake.

"Thank you. It took a lot of effort … believe me."

"I know, and they all look so sophisticated. How do you do it?"

"Technique, I think," she answered, deciding to take the praise. "How is Vasquez?"

"He is fine. Busy on the show. We have our line up tomorrow. You will tune in won't you?"

"Of course, and definitely. I would be delighted to see how he envisions the new normal."

"Great, and I will let him know."

Kascey was still flustered from her ordeal and how she had turned around new designs in such a short period of time. She breathed a sigh of relief. She had learned from the best and was comforted that she had kept up a good mentor–student relationship with Vasquez. It was a very prized mentorship, and the relationship lasted many years and would continue as long as they were able.

5 | A Catskills Lodge

Gradey had placed the belongings in the back of the four-wheel drive as he and Kascey ventured upstate to the lodge in the Catskills for the weekend. It was perched on a little hill with a ravine and large cedar trees. A long trail within the trees led to a ledge overlooking a lake where she and he would hike on summer afternoons. The drive to their new lodge was beautiful with the changing foliage, which turned to bronze, yellow, and red.

"A well-needed break from the city for the weekend," he stated.

"Yes. I have the picnic all packed. What time do you think we should be at the lodge?"

"We should be there in about two hours, depending on the traffic," he reassured her.

"Perfect. I hope that they managed to dust it out. It has been a few months since we made it up."

"Should be fine. Doug had to do maintenance last week."

"Thanks for sorting that. I just had too much to think about."

"I know," he said dismissively, as he had been preoccupied with the new takeover.

"Any word of when we will get to the cape?"

"I think Mum was thinking about late October, while we can still travel and gather. Of course, there are travel requirements to get to the state, like testing and such." On a lighter note, he added, "Time flies; it is already the end of September."

"Yes, I know, it is workable now that I have a breather," she replied.

"Great. I think the operation will be next week, and I'm hoping Aunt Maura can recuperate in time for the weekend. If not, we will have to push it back. By then it will be close to Thanksgiving, and we could spend time with them in Maine anyway. And why expose her unnecessarily." Gradey knew that there were no certainties and that the planning could all change because of travel restrictions.

"That's right," Kascey replied. "I want to spend the holidays with my parents. Remember: they spend the New Year in the islands."

"That sounds like a compromise."

She relaxed during the remainder of the drive. It would not be long before they would be lounging on the porch with cool beverages and packed lunches from the corner gourmet deli. A long romantic hike through the foliage would lead them to the small nearby town, where they could pick up a meal for dinner before dining around the campfire and then settling into the rustic bedroom on her former bachelorette Queen Anne bed and quilted comforter. Her white wicker furniture fit perfectly in the sitting room—an homage to her former NYC Soho bachelorette pad now sneaked away in their holiday lodge.

Gradey parked the car in front of the welcoming and cosy white wooden structure as they climbed out on the rugged pathway to carry their weekend luggage. They climbed the stairs to the porch and to the front door as he decisively inserted the key and turned it. Immediately as they walked in, there was a lovely bouquet of her favourite flowers of the season sitting on the small dining table.

"Thank you. When did you manage this?" Kascey remarked.

"You are welcome. I must admit that Doug arranged it from the village," he admitted.

"Chrysanthemums, tracheliums, baby's breath, and lilies. How beautiful," she said as she approached to examine them and delicately leant over to inspect as the aroma became more distinct.

She placed the food package on the table and continued to the stairs to the bedroom.

"It is all so clean," she exclaimed, admiring her surroundings.

"We really have to thank him. It must have been in some shape."

"I know. Thankfully it leaves less for me to do. We can just relax and have a bite, as it is twelve thirty already," she said.

"Sure. Just let me unwind. Do you want a protein shake or beverage?" he asked.

"Just a shake, and then we can have a little picnic out front," she suggested.

"Yes, while the weather is still good. Just a nippy fall breeze out. But in the winter the porch is covered with snow."

"Aww, it is just us and nature. Look at the view of the lake from the window," she said.

"Beautiful. The fall foliage is really setting. Those leaves have changed rapidly this year."

"Yes. It is as if they know what the year has been like," she confessed.

Gradey sat on the bed and bounced on it a little, remembering the times together in the city when they were dating.

"Come have a seat," he suggested as he cracked open his drink.

"Ahh, it still feels so good," she said, relaxed as she plunged on the sofa beside him. "Are you hungry?" she asked.

"Not just yet," he said as he placed his arm around her shoulder.

~~~~~

Kascey had ordered some tomato-and-pesto panini and Waldorf salad from the deli, along with other salads as snacks to consume later. There were also several pints of chocolate chip cookie dough frozen yogurt. There was a leftover frozen organic pizza which she would not even attempt to discover. It had been a long time of not having the privilege of such food, and they intended to relish every flavour that they had been unable to experience for some time. They sat outside on the porch and took in the fresh autumn air while they sipped drinks, ate, and laughed. The strong afternoon sun beat down from its highest point before its recline. They walked off the logy feeling of their meal by hiking to the village.

They walked closer, and the quaint convenience store came into view. It was well stocked with local goods and gourmet delicatessen items. It had the semblance of an extensive swank NYC deli and was where they stocked up for the weekend. Kascey wandered the aisles like an excited teenager on a summer camp trip, piling things in the cart to purchase.

"Are we taking some of that stuff back with us?" Gradey asked, surprised.

"I figured that we would in case it becomes hard to get around in the city again. I am relishing this experience of being in the store. There is hardly anyone in here."

"Yes. A little bit of freedom."

Kascey enjoyed being able to anonymously let her hair down after the months of keeping safe and staying in the apartment. They purchased the items at the counter and walked out with brown paper bags.

While strolling back along the small streets, they could see their little lodge perched on the hill along a winding driveway.

"Here is our cosy home," she commented.

"Our charming house. This hill is a bit steep though," he answered.

"Yes, a bit steep. Good exercise though. I figure that we burned enough calories to enjoy that frozen yogurt tonight."

"Sure did. Are you getting good reception on your phone?'

"Not really. Why? Are you expecting a call?"

"No, not really," he responded nonchalantly. However, he was yearning to check on the new deal at work.

"Relax, remember," she said.

"Yep." He was short, having other issues on his mind, such as trying to find a signal.

The afternoon wore on as they soaked up the last of the sunshine. Soon the evenings would start to get colder, and the sun would hibernate in the afternoons for the winter, while the grass on the front lawn would turn crisp from the frost.

Gradey lit a small campfire so that they could roast vegetables and s'mores and sit beside it until the sun set and it had become dark in the back lawn. The lanterns on the pillars of the house then lit automatically to illuminate the exterior of the house.

"When will be the next time that we will be able to do this?" she asked.

"Not for a while. Unless we come up one more time before Thanksgiving."

"Not even then. Have I told you how much this whole experience has meant to me with you being there?"

"No." He smirked and bit into a french fry.

"Well it does. I could not have done this without you. This pandemic, this isolation … and look how much we have grown—how much stronger we have become because of it," she asserted.

"I am just kidding. Yes, I know what you mean. Usually

we would spend weekends with friends, and that just stopped and it was just us."

"Us two. Would you want three or four?" she asked cautiously.

"I would want as many as you want. We have our whole lives to get this right. I am just enjoying you—your essence and all that I initially fell for and the woman that I know."

"And I am enjoying you and all that you are and all that you can be, and all that you mean to me," she said.

"Yes. It is so true that this can all change, and someday, we will look back on it and wish that we had these times."

"That is right. You know how to be so direct at the right time."

They sat all evening while succumbing to the growing of the evening into night. They had a relaxed conversation until they finally got up, entered the quaint opening to the lodge, and walked up the stairs. Kascey had prepared a warm bath with her favourite oils to comfort her from the chill. The water was warm, and the bath suds brimmed the top of the antique marble bathtub. She lit candles and opened the vast window that overlooked the valley. She could hear the sound of sweet jazz while Gradey sat downstairs sipping the last of the pinot grigio as he waited for her.

"All right dear?" he said as she stepped out and downstairs.

"It's all right now," she answered. "I am sad that the weekend has come to a close and we have to get back to the city tomorrow." She would be faced again with her troubles. For now it was just the two of them.

"Just think about this time and this peace. Nothing can harm us; you have me," he reassured her.

He was one of the things that she had initially bet on as working out and had counted as precious. "I am delighted," she responded. She had distracted her mind from the problems at work with a wonderful weekend in the Catskills.

They dozed off in her former bed in the silk sheets at about midnight and woke in heavenly euphoria from the night before. Their relationship had now grown to new heights. It had matured as the summer had created a new variation to their relationship. There were no family and friends—just two people surviving the effects of the pandemic. They counted only on themselves as the relationship developed.

The following morning, the drive back to the city was calm as they listened to Steely Dan and Fleetwood Mac along the highway. It was just the trip Kascey needed to forget about the hardships of the past months. Outside, the newly formed autumnal hues of the large birches were suddenly behind them as they travelled along the turnpike and then downtown to the greeting of buildings and a quiet Sunday afternoon. Instead of the hustle and bustle of the city, there were newly formed quaint villages and sidewalks. They casually sauntered into their building and across the vast lobby to the elevators, still lugging their belongings. It was if they had gone for a long time.

"You sure have a stack of goodies," Gradey commented.

She blushed at the thought of her convenience store binge. "Yes. Looks like enough to last us for a while."

"Looks like it," he said with a grin.

"It feels good to be back," she said.

"Yes. I have an agenda to complete in the den. I'll join you in a bit."

"Sure. I had better see the studio." She checked the security camera app to check on the studio and then unpacked everything. She cleaned the hiking boots and threw the rest in the wash. "This is such a crisis of the pandemic. I remember when we would send everything to the laundry. Anyway, I will count this as therapeutic," she complained.

"What's that dear?" he called out from the den.

"Nothing. Just figuring this out."

"Okay, dear." He continued on the computer, reading the statements of the new company.

"I think that it will be one of the last good days we get for the early autumn. Come to the terrace and join me. Bring your computer. You can do everything there," she suggested.

"I'll be right out. I just need a minute while I note this thought."

"All right. I have pasta prepared." She placed it on the tablecloth along with utensils and red wine. It was a special recipe from her mother, Mabel.

They sat on the terrace as the sun began to dip below the horizon of the bay. "Beautiful today," she commented.

"Sure is. I really must thank you for such a beautiful weekend. This meal is perfect. I will always remember this weekend."

"It was fantastic. I can't bear to think of the week ahead."

"I know. It will all turn around. Remember what I said."

"I remember." She sipped some more wine and offered him the dessert.

6 | Weekend at the Cape

Snugly ensconced along the winding shoreline of the Cape was Silent Manor. Edged behind the sand dunes with a light blue exterior and a family porch stood the four-bedroom beach house of the Chisol family. Kelly and Damian had bought it when Gradey and Lucy were children, and it had been a holiday home for decades. It was managed by their loyal housekeeper, Jane, who was like a member of the family. They had hosted all their children's friends, and it was a place where Gradey and Kascey would visit while engaged with friends. It was where they spent Labor Days, which they had missed this year.

Kelly and Damian arrived first, with Kelly's sister, Aunt Maura. She looked similar to her sister but had red hair. Once she had completed a major operation, she had gained some strength. Her recuperating body was wrapped in a winter coat, and she had lost her jovial charm from the ordeal. It was a compliment to her more conservative and dutiful sister. It was Maura who could bring out the excitement and was energetic. She had had a short marriage, and since she had no children, her niece and nephew were her focus.

They aided her from the car as her nurse, Mitsy, carried

her belongings to the house. Mitsy was staying in town and would spend days at the house during the weekend. Kelly tended to her every need as if there was no need for anyone else. They entered the house and settled in the sitting room. It was furnished in its familiar white beach furniture and cream walls. There were glass tables and striped beach cushions and rugs. It had a rustic aquatic feel, as it was suitable for tracking in sea salt and sandy feet.

"Jane," called Kelly, "how are you doing? What do you have prepared for today?"

"Fine, thanks. A whole feast, Mrs. C. I have spent the whole morning on the children's favourites." She had been a reliable staple in the family during their hosting as teenagers their friends from school as well as their new tastes. She had been shopping all day yesterday and had several delights prepared. "I have the corn fritters and tempura vegetables for Luce with her special dip, and I have been barbecuing for Gradey. There is pot pie and lemon pie, as well as pumpkin pie, autumn vegetable soup, and salad."

"Sounds fabulous," Kelly said. "Have you done all that work? It smells delicious." She neared the kitchen to inspect it all while Damian took the luggage to the bedroom.

Lucy and Nate were the next to arrive and had taken the precautions required to cross the state and to cover up if warranted. It was a COVID-free environment before a second wave, and they had to be tested to spend time with their aunt. They were reticent, as was Gradey, to even attend. Married life had suited Lucy, as she had put on a few pounds. The couple had enjoyed a quiet wedding the previous Easter with a few close family during the pandemic. Kelly and Damian had promised a large party when the restrictions had lifted the following year to celebrate properly.

"Mum, Jane, how are you both?" she said as she greeted them.

"Much better," admitted Kelly, careful not to let her voice travel to the sitting room. "You look well, actually as if you have put on a few pounds."

"Just a little, Mother," she replied feeling self-conscious.

"Hello, and simply fine. Well, you are looking very well. I have prepared a few of your favourites," Jane replied appeasingly.

"Thanks, and that is great. I am looking forward to it."

"Where's Nate?" asked Kelly.

"I am right here. Just getting a few things out of the car. Hello, Mrs. C., how are you?" he asked politely and empathetically.

"Much better, dear, now that Maura is out of the hospital."

"That is good to hear. Where is she?"

"She is right in the sitting room if you all want to say hello before settling."

"Yes, that would be great," replied Lucy as she steered her husband to the sitting room.

"Well, Jane, I am going to get settled, and we can have lunch at one thirty after Gradey and Kas arrive."

"I'll have it all prepared, and don't worry about a thing."

"Thank you."

Gradey and Kascey pulled up to the sleepy driveway of the manor. It was lodged behind the beach. Gradey parked the vehicle, and they disembarked, hauling their bags with them. The beach house had a different feel in late October. The sun was not as high, and the chill was almost like winter with the cool sea breeze. It was almost evening and they had been on the road all morning.

"That drive was actually longer than expected." Gradey noted.

"I know; we are just in time for lunch, and barely," she responded.

"That is all right. There was a little more traffic, and I am sure that they will understand."

"Yes, of course," Kascey replied concerned. "I just don't like to be late."

"I know. It's fine."

Grady was more relaxed than Kascey, as they were dealing with his family and she did not want to take the blame.

They walked in to find Jane in the kitchen. "Well, hello," she called out as she heard the door slam.

"Hi, Jane. It has been some time," responded Gradey, incredibly happy to see her.

"I know. A very strange year, and it is good to see you," she replied reminiscent of former days with him. "How are you, Kascey?"

"Fine, thank you, Jane. It's wonderful to see you again. I see you are busy preparing everything."

"Yes, and it is great to see you. The others have just settled in, and your Aunt Maura is in the sitting room."

"Great. I can't wait to see her. How does she look?" Kascey asked with concern as Gradey listened intently.

"She looks rather well. It has been a few weeks since the operation."

"I know. We are so lucky that she made it through," Gradey replied.

"We certainly are," she agreed.

Gradey and Kascey passed through the kitchen to the sitting room to greet his aunt. She was seated with her drip, and it was evident she had lost a few pounds. She was wrapped a beige wool pashmina and wore tan woollen trousers and a cream silk shirt. It appeared that she was on the road to full recuperation, which relieved them, as she appeared bright and healthy.

"Aunt Maura. So lovely to see you. You look well," Gradey greeted.

"Hello, Gradey. It is lovely to see you too. We got the message that you were stuck in traffic. I hope that it was not too much trouble to get here," she replied graciously.

"No trouble at all. None at all."

"Hello, Aunt Maura, it is great to see you doing better. How are you feeling?" asked Kascey.

"Look at you. Such a wonderful blouse. I am feeling much better, thank you. It is a breezy day, and I can feel a little of the chill from the seaside."

"I see. Well, perhaps we can close a few more windows or put the heating up," suggested Gradey.

"If that would be better," she replied appreciatively. She had spent many years in the house, and this was a new complaint. The cool autumn had set in, and it was almost Thanksgiving and late in the year to be gathering at the house, which was usually used for the summer months.

"We will come back in a minute. Just going to get settled out back."

"Sure, and take your time. I think that Jane will help me once she is through in the kitchen." It was a new protocol. Usually she was like the rest. However, she needed to be guided in by two people.

"Not a problem, I can help get you in there," suggested Gradey.

He motioned to the nurse, and they gently lifted her by the arms out of the sitting chair. It was a slow and steady walk to the room. They then placed her on the bed.

"I will just go and get your things," he promised.

Kascey had started to bring in the overnight bag and handed it to Gradey. "Here we go. Where shall I put this?"

"Just next to the bed to sort out. Thank you." She was pleased and knew that when her striking and gallant nephew arrived, she would be more reinforced. She yearned to heal and to get back to normal.

Kascey and Gradey settled into the guest bedroom overlooking the water. It was a beautiful autumn day. The shoreline was breezy and dark for this time of the year. They could hear the seagulls and the brush of the waves on the shore along with the rustling of the wax myrtle and sea oats.

"She looks well," commented Kascey, relieved.

"Yes, thankfully. It has taken her a while to get to this point, and I am glad that she is out of the pain."

They heard a knock. "Come in," answered Gradey, knowing who it would be.

"Hello dear, Kascey. Are you all settled in okay? How was your drive down?"

"Mom. Good. Hello," Gradey replied. "It feels like ages, Mom, and the trip was smooth. Longer than thought." He looked at Kascey, who concurred.

"Yes, we got in a bit of traffic on the way down. So sorry to be a little late."

"Not a problem. We are all just settling in. Have you everything you need? More towels? Anything else, just let us know." She still pampered him and asserted her position as host, as if he and Kascey were coming in for a college holiday trip.

"Sure thing, Mom," he answered.

"Thanks, we are fine for now," replied Kascey rather obligingly.

"Great. Have you seen your aunt?" she asked before leaving.

"Yes. We just moved her to her room. She looks very well."

"I know," she whispered at the doorway, trying to keep her tone down. "Such a blessing that she is recovering so well. She has been through a lot. Anyway, we shall see you all at lunch in half an hour."

"Thanks. See you in a bit, Mom," Gradey replied, edging her on a bit so that they could settle in before then.

Kascey unzipped her roller bag and took out a few items of clothing.

"You are not changing, are you?" he asked.

"Not right now; this is for dinner," she replied.

"I see." He was used to her wearing different outfits throughout the day even for an intimate weekend trip to the cape.

"Darling, don't you know that it is what I do?" she replied, knowing full well what he was thinking. Her way of dressing was slightly more sophisticated, her having been raised in a family who concentrated on fabrics and clothing.

They strolled out to the dining room and saw that everyone was assembling and taking their seats.

"Just sit anywhere. We will socially distance ourselves," suggested Kelly.

"Kascey, Gradey, how have you been?" asked Lucy.

"We are doing fine. It has been too long," answered Gradey.

"Yes, too long, Lucy. Nate, how are you?" added Kascey.

"Very well. Glad that things are picking up in retail," he admitted.

"I know. It must have been exceedingly difficult for you all," empathized Gradey.

"To say the least," he replied.

"I think that we are out of the woods for now; it has been horrendous," Gradey agreed.

"Luce, you seem to have put on a few pounds since I saw you last," said Gradey.

"Just a little," she said as she looked at Nate, pleased.

"What? Are you serious?" asked Gradey.

"What's that, hon?" asked Kelly while Jane busily brought the dishes out to the buffet table.

"Everyone please help yourselves and sit anywhere." Jane said, sweeping an arm before her. "Maura, let me get your plate for you."

"Eat up, everyone, before it gets cold," added Kelly.

"This all looks wonderful," observed Damian.

"It certainly does," commented Kascey.

They all got their meal and tucked in. "Now, Lucy, you were saying something," said Gradey.

"Yes, Nate and I are expecting."

"You are?" asked Damian.

"Yes, we are," she replied ecstatically.

"Congratulations, honey. That is beautiful, isn't it, Damian?"

"Wonderful, Lucy. I am so pleased."

"Congratulations Luce, Nate," answered Gradey.

"That's wonderful. How far on are you, if I may ask?" asked Kascey.

"Thanks. We are about three to four months. The baby should be born by February."

"Congratulations, dear. That is wonderful news," chimed in Aunt Maura.

"Thank you, Auntie," she replied, pleased.

"I am so happy for you both. We are going to be grandparents," stated Kelly, knowing full well that they would be taking on a new role that she would embrace thoroughly. "Such a blessing," she continued.

"Yes, dear. That is great news," replied Damian proudly.

Gradey felt a hint of exclusivity. He was incredibly happy for her and wondered when it might happen for him. Kascey had been so busy with work and was coming out of an ordeal, so he knew that now was not the right time. However, now that Lucy had got the ball rolling, he felt as though there should be company.

The family enjoyed the rounds of courses as Jane proudly brought them out. They were truly celebrating and had their blessings to count. There had been a successful operation, and a new addition was coming to the family. Kelly had her Thanksgiving early and all for which she had hoped. It was a weekend of catching up and reminiscing over how life was and could be again, as there was no certainty as to when things would be the same again.

Dinner followed in much the same relaxed fashion, and Sunday brunch followed. It was a weekend of quality time overlooking the depths of the water's edge and a new phase: a new season, a new lifestyle, and a new member of the family.

Kelly was overjoyed about what life was like after the last few months. "We say that it is difficult to start again. I think that we have been lucky for a chance at new beginnings. We can dwell on the past year and all that has been lost, and we can later pick up the pieces and learn how to overcome it all to make a new future—a stronger and brighter one. Let us not forget all that we have been through, but use it as a tool to rebuild a new foundation of what this family can be again."

"I second that dear," Damian replied with a toast. The meal was not overindulgent and included a roast with potatoes followed by a trifle pudding. Afterwards, still overcome with celebrating, they laughed, played board games, and watched the TV in the sitting room. They spent time talking about old times: when they were children or were visiting from college, and the last wedding in the islands.

"Another successful day, hon," commented Damian as they retired to their quarters.

"I could not have asked for anything better. A perfect day, hon," she replied.

The wind strengthened over the course of the evening, and a cool chill set in from the ocean as it grew darker. The younger generation had settled in, as it was almost midnight. Kelly and Damian sauntered to their bedroom, delighted about the events of the day and that it almost seemed that everything was back to normal.

~~~~~~~~~~~~~~~

Kascey and Gradey had an early start back to the city. The drive was silent when Gradey asked her, "Would you want children anytime soon?"

"I do, but I really have to get the business established first. It is such an easy time to fit having a child in now with the slowdown, but I am anticipating that things will start up again."

"Whatever you decide, I am okay with it. I was just wondering if you felt a little slighted by Lucy's announcement?" he asked, sounding concerned.

"Not at all. It makes me want to get started, but I have no real time frame. I am still only twenty-nine. I have time."

"Yes you do. I am okay with it if you are."

"I'm okay right now," she said. Deep down, she did feel a yearning and looked forward to when she could have a child, but it was not on the cards at the moment.

It was a bright and cool day. The drive was scenic and golden as they passed along the trees, whose hues were changing for autumn.

"This is one of my favourite times of the year. It is full of renewal and change," Kascey commented.

"I think it is so beautiful out here." They passed through Connecticut on their way to the city at about noon. "We have been driving for almost two hours and should be in the city by two depending on the traffic."

"That is fine. I am just enjoying the time with you. Do you want a snack?" Kascey asked as she pulled out some treats that Jane had packed.

"Not right now. Save me some though."

"Of course, I am not going to eat it all," she clapped back.

"I know, just teasing, all right?" He replied sarcastically.

"Aren't you relieved that Maura looked so well?" she asked.

"Totally. I am really thrilled about that. It was really

weighing on me. We have such a small family, and for anything to happen to her would be such a loss."

"Well, she has been spared," she said hopefully.

"Yes. Thankfully."

The city was not as crowded as it would be at this time of day on a Sunday. Many people were still practising social distancing, and there were still hospitality restrictions. She got out of the car at the entrance of the building before he went to park the car. The door attendant, Lester, obligingly helped her with the luggage as she went to the apartment. She could feel the stress increase as she entered to her existing problem and the teleconferences that she had Monday.

Gradey took a while to enter the apartment with the remainder of the bags. "Hi, I got caught up on the phone."

"Really? With whom?"

"Claude had been trying to reach me regarding the trade. Nothing that we cannot deal with at the office tomorrow."

"I see." She looked perplexed, not wanting to push any more.

"Right then. Shall we order some lunch or dinner? It is pretty late."

"Yes. Something simple. Whatever you wish, dear."

They spent the rest of the evening lounging and reflecting on the events of the weekend. Being back in the familiar sprawling bungalow ensconced along the shore and with spectacular views of the cape had grounded them. They reminisced on its fiery orange sunsets and bright blue days, along with the fresh sea air and vast horizon.

7 | A Safe Monday

Kascey had fully returned to her studio near Midtown, which was not far from the apartment. It was a bright autumn morning, so she walked several blocks. It was still infused with the aroma of new carpeting and paint as she entered and took the elevator up to the twelfth floor. The studio loft was compartmentalized, with long tables for fabrics and sofas and lounge chairs for clients. Her staff had arrived and were busy at their computers, diligently starting the new day.

"Morning all. You are all here so bright and early," she said.

"Morning. Yes we have those holiday orders now," replied Judee.

"Great. How is it looking?" Kascey asked as she unwrapped her scarf and took off her coat.

"Sales are picking up. A little lower from last year, but enough sales I think," Judee speculated.

"That sounds promising. Can you send me the figures?" asked Kascey.

"Sure thing."

"How was your weekend?" asked her assistant, Syre, noting enthusiasm in her step.

"It was wonderful. We spent the weekend at the cape with Gradey's family and got to see everyone. It was socially distanced and really safe," she explained.

"That sounds great. How was his aunt?"

"Actually, we are quite pleased. She is recovering quite well," she replied.

"That's good news. You must be so relieved."

"Yes, we are, and Lucy is expecting."

"Wow! That is fantastic," added Judee.

"Yes, I know, and we are all so happy for her."

"Perfect. Does that mean that she will leave Marleys?" Judee asked.

"Well, not right now, but I am sure they will have to sort that out when the baby arrives. Wow! I can't believe what I am saying. When the baby arrives, I will be an aunt."

"That is perfect. Congratulations," said Syre.

"Thank you," she said proudly. She had known Luce longer than she had known Gradey. She had been at a launch party, and Luce, who was a buyer of her former boss's couture, introduced her to Gradey, her brother. She always appreciated that gesture and considered her an ally forever.

"Now, I am just going to go through the sales statistics for the season." She flicked through the files and some of her emails. She saw one from Valentino, her technician. He had attached the details of the incident in a statement to send to the lawyers about the sordid ordeal. A website with some of her fake designs had been found, and a trace had been performed to locate the responsible party, apparently from extremely far away. It was customary for the culprits of the scheme to change their operation several times to avoid being detected. Kascey felt a sense of relief that they had been discovered. She sent the email to her lawyer, Norsa, on whom she had become dependent, not only because she had provided good service but also because she was quick and thorough. She made Kacey feel as though she was appreciated, and she soothed her concerns.

Kascey noticed that Norsa had replied to her email:

> Thanks for this information. We are working on this and will have subpoenas and cease orders issued tomorrow for the breach of cybersecurity and data theft. A Signorio Mestes Partners Inc. was on the writ. The amount of damages has risen to $12 million. You have suffered enough stress and loss from this as well as instituted a contingency plan to save your existing business and brand. There is a great chance of success, as this has been litigated before and they are no strangers to the long arm jurisdiction of the law.

Kascey breathed a sigh of relief. The morning was unfolding in the right way. She could get back to the business of designing in her own socially distanced environment with her trusted staff. The dresses for the holidays were flamboyant, in greens, reds, fuchsias, and purples. They were buoyant and flowing for the festive season, which most people would be spending at home or at private gatherings around the world. It was fair to conclude that the holidays had arrived with a different mood. It was emotional, and she felt that it was more special and sentimental. She wanted her customers to remember the holiday season without the sadness, not only because of its significance but also as a badge of overcoming misery. She wanted to scrub the misery away and look forward to a brand-new year.

She called Gradey. "Hi, dear. How is your Monday?"

"How is my Monday? Well, it is a little mundane. I needed a break. How is yours?"

"It is starting off on the right footing. You know, I am so happy that I listened to your advice about the lawyer. She is a godsend. She has found the thieves and is now issuing the summonses for the case. It is so relieving. How did they even get a hint of me? They are so far away."

"I know. So she has that all under control? I knew it. She is so highly recommended. I mean, look how she handled the last injunction for Vasquez. It is such a relief to have people you can rely on during times like this." He reassured her.

"Indeed. Anyway I just wanted to wish you a perfect day."

"Thank you, dear, and talk to you soon." Gradey replied.

<hr />

Gradey disconnected and stared at the financial statements for Tirogam. It was not looking good. To get the boost, there would need to be more capital investments and some losses.

It was hard to figure it all out. A trip to Silicon Valley was warranted—and soon, while travel was still possible, as there was talk of curfews and a shutdown over the season.

"Norma, could you look at my schedule and let me know when we can fit in a trip to California before Thanksgiving? After that, it might not be possible for a few months."

"Yes. Sure. Let me see … I think the week before would be perfect, and we can get you back to the city on the red-eye that Wednesday, the nineteenth."

"Great. What time, because we need to leave for Maine? Or should I just go straight there?"

"You could do that. I mean, Kascey could take a flight that afternoon and still meet you there."

"Yes, that might be better. To get to the city, we might get stuck, and the weather might be bad anyway, and there are new restrictions."

"Okay. Let me get the travel arrangements confirmed for you. I will send you the itinerary. And shall I look into flights for Kascey?"

"No, that is fine. I am sure she will be in a better position to know what she really wants—I mean once she gets there on time." He hung up knowing that it might be difficult to get around at that time of the year. It was the most hectic flying time, and there were challenging social distancing rules and restrictions in place. She might want to hire a private emission-free plane, which would be cheaper if he were to do the same thing from California for him.

He had to take care of the company issue. "Claude, we

have to plan the trip to Silicon Valley that's coming up in a few weeks."

"I would prefer sooner," he replied.

"Fine," Gradey said, "why don't you go in now and then we go back in a few weeks to close the deal. I mean, it will be a very sorry holiday season. It would be best if we could just hold on until after Thanksgiving with any cuts. The situation is grim enough without adding to it."

"Sure. I can make it after the elections the first week of November."

"Perfect. No need to tell me how you will vote," he lightly said.

"No, I am sworn to my own secrecy," Claude professed.

"Okay."

He knew that he would jump the schedule planning to get things started. It was his personality. At least they had jumped the hurdle of being in separate homes and were in the same office. He still felt personally distant from his colleagues after the time apart and all the experiences and losses that had occurred. Gradey got his scenic view back in the office, which brought optimism and a reminder of how he built his career the first time and would rebuild now. It was a view that meant that he could do whatever it took to make it. On a clear day he could see most of downtown and the Brooklyn Bridge. He had arrived at the city with dreams and made them big. He'd had luck his entire life, and he hoped that this was no exception. He considered himself to be a lucky man. He had landed the job after searching and pounding the pavement on interviews.

He had met the woman of his dreams and lived the perfect life after having survived the first wave of the pandemic. It had all brought about a tinge of guilt. He felt guilty about how they had managed to survive while so many perished. He needed to talk it out and would phone his father later. He was always there to help.

He had met the woman of his dreams and lived the perfect life after having survived the first wave of the pandemic. It had all brought about a tinge of guilt. He felt guilty about how they had managed to survive while so many perished. He needed to talk it out and would phone his father later. He was always there to help.

Kascey reminisced about when she and Gradey were newly engaged and enjoyed lunches together, which she missed. She was always so busy in the studio, and he was stuck in the office, and then the pandemic occurred to flatten everything. They made up for it with intimate lunches in their dining room or on the terrace, but things were starting to pick up and they had not done it in a while. It was soon time for date night again. They would have an outdoor evening in October before it got too cold and while still possible. Halloween was upon them, and after that the weather would plummet.

She scoured her phone for ideal places to meet outside over the next few days. A romantic late lunch would be just what they needed. There was a surge of excitement on Fridays when she knew that they would be meeting. She could hardly get through those days and had such incentive after a long week. The invigorating Friday environment on the cusp of a weekend surrounded them in their swanky bistros as happy hour set in. She reminisced about the novelty of their relationship and wanted that spark.

"Back to work," she murmured. She flicked through the

fake website offering her designs. She felt as though she were eerily looking at a mirror image of her soul. Her heartfelt designs had been lifted and replicated. The beige-and-cream loungewear was draped on unknown models and on racks. The lovely evening gown she had saved for her close friend, Moda, was being showcased in a ridiculously cheap and unsophisticated way unbecoming to the regality of the dress. Her designs were not the only ones. The culprits had a habit of ripping off celebrities. She never thought of herself as such, but she supposed that she was considered a business personality. It made no difference once her work received recognition.

"I can't believe this," she said to Judee.

"What is that?"

"Look at these rip-offs."

"What?" she replied rushing over. "Ohh no. Are those the designs?" she asked, trying to compose herself.

"Yes. You can surely tell. This has to be stopped," Kascey insisted.

"I know. How awful," she replied sadly.

"Right then. I am going to call the lawyer to have this stopped. They should not be doing this while the case is ongoing."

"I know. Good move. You must remember that we are not dealing with the conventional. These people are criminals, so they will probably just hide away until they re-emerge," reasoned Judee, knowing that these cases were difficult to regulate.

"You are probably right. We can probably wound their operation in any event. Something is better than nothing."

"I know," Judee agreed.

"I was ahead of them and got some new designs out that they could not replicate in time. That is when you are the original."

"Yes, you are right," Judee said, encouraging Kascey. "This definitely has to stop."

It was more than a mundane Monday. She had accomplished so much and was proud of her staff for adjusting to the new normal. The business had taken on a new outlook. It would be that way for some time. It was already 6.00 p.m., and the sun had lowered and the autumnal breeze had set in. Kascey was on her way home as she prepared herself for the familiar streets. She had a home that she had created with her new husband, and she felt complete again. She switched off the lights and locked the studio before descending in the lift and exiting the swanky red brick building.

When she entered her condominium apartment, she found her husband having a cocktail on the sofa, relaxing with his tie undone.

She walked over, removed her face mask, and leant over and kissed him. "Hello, dear."

"Hello. What was that for?"

"Nothing. Just saying hello. How was your day?" she asked as she nestled close to him.

"Um, I'd rather not say. A bit tricky, to say the least."

"Sorry to hear it," she replied, having an idea of what it was like.

"Oh, by the way, I am travelling the week of Thanksgiving to sort things out before travel becomes restricted. You might have to get to my folks on your own. Is that okay?"

"Sure it is. Why have you chosen to travel then? A bit hectic, right, and we do now know what the regulations might be?"

"I know. It has to be done, and I can't take the grief right now. I wish that I had a solution and could postpone it," he replied sharply.

"Sorry. Do you want to have something to eat?"

"Yes. Sure. What's on order?"

"I guess some sushi or something."

"Right, that would be great, thanks. Just get what you want, and I'll have some."

"Sure." She could not deal with him when he was so detached. It was his response to stress. She decided to put up with it as saving grace. *He just needs a few hours of reflection*, she thought.

It was a tepid evening and not as she had hoped. She really needed to get the flair back in the relationship and brighten his spirits.

"Why don't we have lunch on Friday? Like old times?" she suggested.

He sipped his drink and candidly placed it down while thinking. "Sure. Whatever you want."

"Good. I will sort it out and lighten up. Will I have to spend the entire evening like this?"

"All right. Sorry. I just have so much on my mind, and it is making me make decisions that I would not otherwise. Come here," he said as he held her closer.

"It's all right, dear."

They cuddled for the rest of the evening on the settee and had their favourite meal delivered. Time was precious and not worth the waste of temperamental issues as they thought of how to navigate through what appeared to be more harrowing times with the prospect of new optimism around the corner.

8 | Weekend Buzz

The energy in the studio had mounted, and the studio was abuzz with the anticipation of the weekend. Not only was it Friday; it was Halloween—albeit a sedate one in the city. Lunch date day had finally arrived, and Kascey, bursting with enthusiasm, was dressed in a vintage black dress with pearls and satin gloves. It was a semblance of an homage to Holly Golightly for Halloween. She covered her ensemble with a large faux-fur white coat—a contrast to the outdoors, as the weather had turned to its habitual grey fall morning as it grew darker earlier. Syre and Judee were dressed similar to the Great Gatsby and Jean Harlow in an early-twentieth-century motif.

Kascey had picked a swank french bistro with rave reviews for lunch. They had planned a late lunch in the Flatiron District, which then poured into happy hour. The city had a hint of normalcy, as she had a challenging time with the limited indoor seating. She had thought of driving out of town, but it was just lunch, and they would soon, she hoped, be in Maine for the weekend.

"Don't forget; I am leaving work early today," she reminded her staff.

"That's right, you have fancy plans. We will happily keep the fort while you are gone," replied Judee.

"Thanks. It will be a late lunch. I leave at about two." Kascey replied. "Any plans this weekend?"

"Yes. Socially distanced plans at a friend's house on Long Island for Halloween. A small gathering—and just as much fun, I hope."

"Sounds fantastic! Stay safe—although I do not need to warn you." Kascey missed the fancy plans. She felt a different sentiment to her married life and was focused on her relationship. Her colleagues were also newlyweds or into raising their children, and her school friends in Canada were all settled in homelife in the suburbs. She had since moved and fully ensconced herself into her new country, as she had relocated years ago and had built so much in the city. It was a remarkably familiar place, as she had made many visits to the city as a child with her parents.

"I see it that it's almost time I leave. Do not forget to lock up." She said as she dashed out the door and pulled her coat around her. Her black boots skidded on the tile as she caught herself on the way to the elevator.

"Bye! Have fun!" Judee called out. "Happy Halloween!"

"Have a great weekend, and Happy Halloween!" followed Syre.

"Thanks," Kascey said as she pushed the ground floor button of the elevator.

The ride down was swift, and she hailed a cab to get to the bistro. When she arrived, she had to complete a few details on a form, and she was seated under the awning near the back and next to the window. It reminded her of so many evenings in Paris with Gradey. She waited for him, and he was late by about fifteen minutes when she glimpsed his familiar face rushing in.

"Hi, hon, sorry I'm late," he apologized cheekily as he leant over to give her a kiss.

"Hello. That is all right. I only just got here," she greeted him sweetly.

"Good," he said as he took a seat extra close to her. "Do you want to order a bottle of wine?"

"Sure. Are you not going back to work?"

"No, I am finished. Besides, it is evening on the Continent," he replied snidely.

"Whatever you want. They have such a delightful menu here."

"Good. Have whatever you want." He was very pleasant. It was a semi-holiday after all, and they had been budgeting for six months. "I guess that a little splurge for the joys of marriage won't hurt."

"I guess. Now what do you think you will have?"

"The usual. Is it on here?" he asked, taking a closer look.

"Yes, I have checked," Kascey replied. "Chicken fricassee, pasta, or steak and frites?"

"I think the pasta, thanks. And you?"

"Right then. I would like the ratatouille. Promise you will share a crème brûlée."

"Sure," he said as he perused the wine list. "Can we also fit in a chocolate soufflé?"

"Great. I'll have some." After a month of working out and budgeting, they were able to indulge once again while the novelty lasted.

"Okay, and that is sorted. Where is the waiter?" It appeared he had negotiated a perfect lunch and had not left the office. He peered around the establishment, which was quiet. "I see that the waiter is outside tending to patrons. Service is going to be a bit slow," he realised.

"Things are not back to normal, I guess," Kacey replied. "Not to worry. We can catch up on plans in a few weeks."

She did not want a few glitches to ruin either their meal together or the precious time that they had taken. The atmosphere was still lively despite the few patrons with the full ambiance. The chequered tablecloths had been replaced, and the menus were disposable. She admired that the payment was contactless as they left credit card details for the booking online. "Let's not mar the moment with triviality. What is important is what we have here and this special time." She said this despite knowing that they had spent months together cooped up in the condo.

Gradey was satisfied with his meal as they shared their desserts. It was half past four, and happy hour had begun. As it was Halloween, and crowds started to gather outdoors on the pavement. "I think that we should take that gesture and make a move. Social distancing is still imperative, since we will be seeing family in a few weeks' time."

"Sure. Understood," she said. "Let's take a cab back. Are you going back to work?"

"No, I will accompany you back. Anything minor can be done at the apartment. I am all yours," he promised. They settled the bill via the online app and gathered their coats and walked out. They shuffled into a cab and enjoyed the smooth and quick ride back to the apartment. The door attendant, Lester, had expected them later and was surprised to see them together so early and gladly opened the entrance for them.

"Afternoon, Mr. and Mrs Chisol," he commented.

"Afternoon, Lester," he replied.

"Yes, afternoon," Kascey said with a smirk.

They strode familiarly to the elevator and up to the apartment. As they walked in, they were greeted by a phenomenal view from the terrace. The sun was setting, and it was almost dark. "I'll be right out as soon as I am done with these new calls." He excused himself.

"Sure, darling. I will just get settled." It was obvious that the spark had reignited and the evening would not be a repeat of Monday. She was smitten with the thought that the outdoors had worked. It was what he had needed to get back to his normal self.

"Good. I won't be long." He disappeared into his den and sat at the computer.

Kascey threw on a silk lounge suit and slippers and selected a film in the sitting room. She arranged some glasses and plates for evening snacks in front of the widescreen TV. She checked her messages and found one from Norsa which had attached to it the copy of the injunction and the subpoena for the case. It was just what she needed to lift her spirits more. It was to inform her that they were set with the injunction and that the papers had been filed. The case was moving on, and it had been a perfect Friday. They could hear a bit of activity on the street from the terrace. After all, there were small celebrations amidst the costumes. There would be times when holiday celebrations would be hindered for safety, as expected, and now it was upon them to navigate a safe evening.

9 | Hope in the Valley

Gradey habitually fastened his seatbelt and secured his mask again. He took an early flight out to the West Coast, which was rumoured to be shut down in a few days. His colleague Claude also took the chance for this last visit for a while and was seated across from him, also taking the necessary precautions.

He felt a tinge of guilt at leaving Kascey during such an important week and wished that he did not have to travel. He kept his fingers crossed, as the weather was forecast for snow at the end of the week. Once airborne, the plane effortlessly glided to the West Coast, passing into a different time zone in advance of Gradey's own.

He became more optimistic as the plane landed on a sunny runway, which contrasted with the climate on the East Coast. They disembarked and entered a very scarce arrivals terminal.

"Where to?" he asked Claude.

"To the hotel in Silicon Valley for a business lunch meeting to go over the statements. I think that it will take a while to get there and back."

"Right. Lots of time to prepare for the meeting. And first up will be Danny Strats, right?"

"Yes. He is the coordinator. And then we meet Roger, the CEO. He is basically the founder of the company. I feel as though middle management might present issues over the downsizing."

"I know, but we have beneficial packages on offer. None of this is good news, but I am sure that they want the company to survive. It is not possible with two hundred employees. I cannot invest any more into it, and it has to turn around," responded Gradey.

"Understood," Claude agreed.

The car arrived at the hotel, where they checked in. Gradey had a massive suite overlooking the Bay Area. He could see the hotel where he spent childhood visits and the familiar routes from his window. For him, the West Coast exuded a certain feeling, and it was the same one he had felt when, as children, he and Lucy anticipated the cable cars, the Fontainebleau Hotel, Disneyland, and Universal Studios. He decided to check in with Kascey to let her know that he had arrived safely.

"Hi, we have made it. How are you?"

"Fine, thanks, and I am glad that you made it. I am just finishing a non-existent lunch break. It is a hectic week; we have sales and holiday order preparations for all over the world."

"I know. The weather is fine here, and look at this view," he said as he turned the phone to the exterior.

"Wow. Big view and big dreams. May they all come true, dear, and good luck," she said, encouraging him.

"Thank you. Had to use my points for it, though. Look, I have to run; the car will be here in ten minutes."

"Right. Miss you, and talk to you soon."

They disconnected with heavy hearts. He knew that he had to travel this week. New York was regular for that time of year, with its cosy and cool temperature. He had a bit of sunshine, but she could not join him. This was purely for work. He knew that she loved the Silicon Valley and had memories of cable cars and a special feeling as a teen visiting with her family.

He descended the elevator and met Claude as they rushed to the saloon waiting outside. It was a long drive out in the heavy traffic. The only issue to overcome was that the city was still on the cusp of the new normal and had further restrictions.

"Things are picking up. There is a risk to travel, and most of the staff are still working from home," Gradey noted.

"Yes, and unfortunately, as they will wish that they could be there."

"I know. Look, we will not go in with a heavy-handed swipe until we have assessed all of the alternatives."

"Right," Claude said, sounding unconvinced.

The car approached an enormous and sprawling building with glass windows and a large recreational park.

"How much property is this?" asked Gradey.

"It must be about two thousand acres."

"Prime location," he replied in awe. We will have to check on the property value. It might be costing more than necessary to run the place because of the size of the facility."

"I would think so. We need to look at the statements."

They disembarked and entered a very swank and modern ground floor lobby with fountains and long reception desks. Before they knew it, they were whisked to the fifteenth floor to see Dan before meeting the CEO, Roger N. Clayt.

"Gradey, Claude, good to see you. How was your trip over?" his voice was welcoming and concerned.

"Great, thanks. Dan, it is good to finally meet you. We had a smooth flight and got in just at the break of day. We had quite a long ride down due to traffic," replied Gradey.

"Well that is good news. Traffic is not half as bad as it could be, because of the downturn. We have a meeting with the boss straight away, and then we can take a tour. There are some offices set up for you to go over the documents, followed by a business meeting with Roger and me this evening, if you are up for it."

"Sure, thanks. We are up for it," Gradey answered.

"Thanks, Dan; we appreciate it," answered Claude. "A bit reassuring to see that it was more active a few weeks ago."

"Yes. Well, we just gave the permission to have more core staff back. As you know, there are a number on furlough."

"I see," said Gradey. "It would be fantastic to meet them at some point in the new year, I know that there are confines right now. It is all about trying to do what is right for them and the company."

"We are reassured that you have joined us. There are some other venture capitalists that would have taken a different stance," replied Dan.

"Count on us," replied Claude.

"I know. We have many alternatives, but I would like to think that I am more humane," said Gradey.

"Good. Now let's go on over to Roger."

Roger was a tech-savvy executive with a relaxed sense of style. His whole energy was unassuming; however, he had managed to build a billion-dollar company. The market had experienced a tech surge, and he saw an increased demand for their services during the pandemic.

Rather impressed, he began, "Well, it sure is great to finally meet you, Gradey. I have heard so much about you. It seems as if we have met already, thanks to all of the times we have had to correspond."

"That is true. It is all part of the business. It is a pleasure working with you."

"Yes, I have met Claude, and I just can't thank you enough for your help with the buyout. We were in dire need of assistance."

"Well, you're welcome," stated Gradey. "It is all part of what we do, and we needed to fit in a trip before the stay-at-home order while trying to be as safe as we can. We just want to have the opportunity to turn the engine around and increase the share price. It might mean making a few choices that are unpopular. I really do not rely on popularity to get me through. We want results, and the company has the potential to turn around. I have seen the statements, and there is a humane way to deal with the staff. If we could just have a better furlough package available for after the holidays, we can increase the profits by spring. The good news is that the economy is on our side, as well as this being an essential business."

"Yes," replied Roger. As an essential, the industry is already recovering. More people used our services than before, and now we are a necessity with the second wave on the horizon."

"That sounds very promising," added Dan. "Might I add that there are so many staff anticipating returning,"

"They still have a job at Tirogam," said Gradey. "However, this is a massive building and operation costs must be through the roof. I see that you have sustainable energy, but there are other factors. Even having to fertilize the lawn is costly, and look at that beautiful landscape."

"Yes, the costs have been great," Roger replied. "You will have a chance to inspect in a few moments. I just wanted to meet you to ensure that we are on the right track. This is still my company; we will just need to work together."

"We are doing that," said Claude, confidently. I think that more will be revealed, and we can discuss more once we peruse the place and the documents."

"Great," Roger replied. "Just remember that we do things a little different in Silicon Valley than on Wall Street. Wall Street benefits from our innovation and unique work culture. I would hate to see that all go to waste,"

"I can reassure you that it will not go to waste," said Gradey. "We want to keep your unique corporate culture. We are proud that you have succeeded based on the millennial concept of unconventional work areas. We will rely on that concept to budget. It will keep this company afloat until the shares increase. I get your corporate mission and objectives. I subscribe to your corporate halo and your sustainability, your belief in human rights, climate change, and zero hunger. All these reasons were an incentive for my reasoning to rescue you. Your people have become my people, and your mission mine. I will keep the culture alive. It is only the residue that I want to cut—the cells that have eroded your concept and your ability to trade like the engine that you deserve to be. When I look at the statements and sit in this office, I want to vicariously live through all that you have fought for and will base my decisions on your journey, not on your definition of the Wall Street concept. The new concept now follows what you have done, and I will survey it with a kind brushstroke and not a sledgehammer."

Claude and Dan looked on in agreement and convinced. Gradey was accustomed to winning and had charismatic skills. He engaged himself in his work fully and had a stern conviction not to contradict his beliefs.

"That is very reassuring to hear. Now let me give you a tour of the place and walk past a few valued staff."

It took over an hour to tour each floor and to greet and wave, socially distanced, at staff. Everyone was masked, and there were arrows and sanitizing stations throughout the floors. A clinic where testing was done was on site. Gradey could detect the apprehension on the staff's faces, and the uncertainty regarding their futures. This moved him, as he wanted to save them and would figure out with the company's concept mission that there was a way to reduce the expenses.

He would achieve this with the belief that benefits would have to be outsourced more cheaply and that there was no way around it.

Gradey and Claude settled in what would be their remote offices for the next three days. There was a feeling of vacancy, as many people were still working from home.

"There is so much information. I am not really sure what time we can leave this evening," Gradey said to Claude, calculating as he perused the files.

"You are right," agreed Claude. "This will take us days. We have until Wednesday. Surely, they can Dropbox some of this."

"Yes. It is sensitive, though. They have competitors who are in the tech industry, and they could easily access this information over the net.

"The exact reason they are able to produce so many security updates for programs. They are always ahead of the game. Decisions, decisions," responded Gradey.

"I know. We will have to make it swift. It is a holiday next week, and I cannot postpone my plans. I think I will propose to Anthea."

"Congratulations, and good luck with that. Have you the ring?"

"I think I will stop by Tiffany's in NYC when we arrive."

"Good. You know Kascey is not being forgiving at the moment. I think wanted to come on this trip."

"Oh dear. True dedication. When you get back, just do something really special."

"Yes. A reconciliation gesture. Anyway, let's get back to business." The two investigated the statements for hours, throwing concepts back and forth. Naturally, Gradey was disappointed with the working capital and capital gains. Also, there was a significant depreciation of assets, and the turnover was low. He contemplated the sale of the building again to which he was growing attached. "How much would you say that this building is worth?"

"I know what they paid," asserted Claude.

"Regardless of that. It has been standing here for almost ten years and needs work."

"I think about one hundred million."

"It is hard to say. We must have it valued. With everyone at home, do they really need it?"

"I don't know," said Claude. "It was a main asset on the books. To liquidate it and then place it into what? It is safer as a tangible. To turn it into liquid capital and disperse it around the assets would cause the overall value of the company to dwindle."

"Not if it needs an injection fast and stands to lose three hundred more million," said Gradey.

"You are right. Save three hundred by sacrificing one hundred. But there must be something else that we can sell, salvage, or cut."

"Right. Let's keep looking."

They continued to pore over the documents, flicking from screen to screen, but the same resolution faced them. It was soon past 5.00 p.m., and they could take this with them to the meeting in a few hours.

"How am I going to figure out how to break it to them that they need to downsize the building?" asked Gradey.

"Exactly like that. However, I would wait until Wednesday."

When evening had fallen, there was an outdoor table booked in the breezy atmosphere overlooking the marina lights of the Bay Area. The restaurant had implemented the outdoor dining details with precautions which were socially distanced and safer. Famished from a long day, they ordered healthy seafood and vegetarian offerings—light fare. Although the financial analysts were exhausted due to jet lag, the main topic to be discussed was the viability of the company to continue as it was and what was needed to solve the problems.

"Thanks for the meal, and I hope that we covered enough business," said Gradey.

"Yes. We really appreciate it in the current climate," added Claude.

"It's the least that we can do, right? I am glad to have you all as partners," replied Roger.

"We are pleased to help. We have many suggestions, but we will leave that for Wednesday. We must get back to avoid the holiday rush and to isolate, but since we are staying close tonight we can afford an early start in the morning. We have not completed our proposal for the scheme and will need more time," Gradey explained.

"Take all the time that you need. We will be working

straight through the holiday, so feel free to get it back to us at any time," confirmed Roger.

"That is very considerate of you. We have an idea of how it will pan out. We just need until midweek. It is reassuring to see your work ethic, and it has been a promising trip which has affected much of our decisions," reassured Gradey.

～～～

The East Coast had a different feel as the November chill set in. Kascey looked at her watch. It was half past eleven, and she had heard from him. The apartment felt empty. She could hear the howling wind as she stared through the open blinds at the full moon. She found it hard to imagine time without him since they met. There were the shows, but this time she felt alone. Had she been with him, she thought of all that they would have done. Her phone buzzed and lit. It was him, finally touching base. "Hello dear, just getting back after dinner. I miss you."

She wrote back, "I miss you too. See you in a few days and chat tomorrow."

Yes. I am exhausted. We are staying near the bay to get some work done. Cheerio.

"Bye, dear," she closed rather sharply.

That was it, a text, after all that she had done to keep the marriage upbeat with the wonderful date lunch and romantic home dinners. She had so much on her plate. She had to deal with the theft of her designs and her business. She felt a little abandoned. She breathed a sigh and tried to recollect positive experiences. She reassured herself that tomorrow, after all, was another day and they had such beautiful times together. She decided to forgive him this one time and move on.

~~~~~~

The sun rose brightly in Silicon Valley on the West Coast. Gradey was ready by 6.00 a.m. PST and wanted to arrive at the office building early. This project was novel to him and was an avenue he had never explored, although he had researched getting a job in the industry when he was starting out. He tried to imagine what his life would have been like had he done so to better understand the position of the corporation and staff. He thought he could almost have been in the same position as Roger with whatever enterprise that he would have started, which impacted his empathy. He phoned Claude to see whether he was available.

"Sure, I am ready. I will call the car to pick us up."

"Right then, I will be right downstairs."

"Okay. See you soon."

It was important to buy something at the staff canteen—not necessarily to explore the menu, but to have a look to determine whether it was an unnecessary cost. The staff had the benefit of an all-inclusive company, which was a definite benefit, and their corporate culture. Gradey was curious as to whether it could be downsized and anticipated inspecting it when he got there.

"Strange that it is November. Look at this; I am in a fall coat. The puffer jacket is back at the suite. I shall certainly be remembering that tomorrow when we get back to the city. It is like thirty degrees."

"We will definitely be needing that," agreed Claude.

They arrived at an impressive scene. The canteen was extensive, with everything for every taste. It seemed like a large warehouse which contained universal variety. It was filled with mostly nutritious options and gluten-free food. Self-service was a requirement so that there was no contact, and he deduced it would also be less costly.

"Are you thinking about how to budget in here?" Claude asked.

"Yes, I am. We have to keep our options open," Gradey admitted.

"I see. I will have a look at the operations report."

"Good idea," Gradey commented. They worked well together and had the same frame of mind when it came to doing business. They soon arrived on the executive floor, where Dan was waiting.

"Morning. Good to see you bright and early."

"Yes. We decided to get an early start as there is so much left to do," Gradey responded.

"Well, if I can be of any help. Just let me know. If not, see you at lunch," Dan replied.

"Right, and thanks. See you later," replied Gradey.

"See you later," Claude added. They were keeping their cards close to them as they walked to their office to finalise the management proposal.

"It is going to be a long day."

"It most certainly is," Claude agreed.

They filed through the documents and analysed the spreadsheets all day. Gradey was inundated with data and new names. He had crammed in so much over the past few days and had meticulously set up a plan. He was not sure that it was agreed, but it was what was needed. He looked at the view of the plush lawns and knew that it would be a long time before anyone would see them in the new year. There would be a total rearrangement after the holidays, and everyone had to be on board. It was imperative to convince Roger and Dan of the outcome. They could restructure and retain the staff, but they had to apply his suggestions stringently, or else it would not work. Gradey had planned to have a jump start by the spring. Drastic measures were to be taken with the stipulation that once the company was profitable, they could have their familiarity again.

It seemed as if time flew due to the hectic events of the day, and Gradey was looking at another evening without Kascey. He sent the proposal to the executives who would present it to the board on Monday. His job was done until then, and it was time for the muted holiday spirit. Gratitude was his motto for the rest of the week because he was able to orchestrate seeing his family when so many could not. He was grateful for the chance to acquire this project and grateful that he could do what was best and not annihilate the stakeholders and the staff because there was so much strife in the year already.

"Hi dear, tell me about your day?" he asked Kascey after a long evening at the office.

"Oh, hi. Well, it went well, and I can't complain. How was yours?" she asked.

"Better than I expected. We fly out tomorrow, and I will get to the hotel in Maine to isolate by four."

"Well, I am looking forward to seeing you soon. I am taking the charter up to Maine. We should have clear weather at least until Thursday."

"Well, I can't wait for the holidays."

"Likewise," she responded.

"Look, I am sorry that I had to plan it all this way. I would much rather have stayed and travelled with you next week. Unfortunately, we had to wrap this project up before the end of the week for the board meeting. I hope that you understand, buttercup."

She laughed at his term of endearment and was distracted from her feigned ruefulness. "Since when have you started to call me that?"

"As soon as I realized that I need you in my life so much. I knew before this trip, and this cements it. No more long trips for the rest of the year. Okay? I promise."

"Promise me and it is a deal. And safe travels tomorrow. Remember to follow the rules so that we can have a safe Thanksgiving."

"Thanks, I will do. I will call you as soon as we get to the airport. I love you."

"Love you too." She had one more day to stick it out. They

had spent so much time together over the last few months that it was unbearable waiting for him. The positive side of the events over the last few months was that they had become closer and stronger.

10 | So Grateful

The leaves in Maine had changed and were falling as Thanksgiving approached. The rustic autumnal hues lay scattered across the ground as the winter chill set in. It was frigidly cold as Kascey stepped out of the airport and entered the car. It was reminiscent of the previous year when she had to travel from the office, and she recognized the difference in her. She felt independent and would not be arriving with Gradey, who was following protocols after his trip. She was truly enthused to see him after a few days apart and would have to contain her excitement because she was meeting other family. Her family in Canada had already celebrated a very dull Thanksgiving in light of the restrictions. Now she could concentrate all her efforts on her new family and the special time building more memories after the very different year.

She bundled up from the chilly air as she leapt from the car to the front door and knocked anticipatingly.

Damian greeted her at the front door. "Hello, Kascey. How are you?" he asked as he walked to her and kept his distance. He reached over and picked up her bag, "Let me get this for you. How was your journey?"

"I am fine, and thank you. It went well considering. How have you been? Not too busy I hope."

"No, and fine, thanks. Jane and Kelly have been in the kitchen preparing for tomorrow, and Maura is in the living room taking a break."

"Fabulous. I can't wait to see everyone. Gradey should be here in about an hour. He was at the airport," she replied.

"Good news," he said as he continued to the bedroom with the bags. "We have refurbished Gradey's old room a bit. I will just set you up in there until he arrives."

"Perfect. Now I will be out in a bit after I freshen up." It was important that she keep her routine after all flights. She had chartered a flight or else would not have arrived in time with the rush and risked other things. A safe environment had been created in the house. She was truly conscientious, knowing that she would have to meet vulnerable relatives; she did not want to put them at risk.

Gradey called to her from the car. "Hello dear. I am just about half an hour away. Miss you."

"Great, and I cannot wait to see you," she said, relieved that he would soon be home. "I am actually in your room, getting sorted."

"Really? Wish that I could be there sooner."

"That is all right; I can manage," she replied.

"Glad that you can remember where to find everything," he replied as the driver kept focused on the road.

"Right, I do, and see you soon. I am heading down to see your mother and aunt soon," she said.

"Good, let them know that I am on my way."

"Sure, honey, and see you soon."

"Bye, see you soon." She knew that he had more to say and would elaborate when he was finally able to see her.

She walked into the kitchen, where the ladies were enthralled with their work. "Kascey. How are you?" asked Kelly, looking up from her pie filling and assessing her structure.

"Fine, thank you. And you?"

"Just busy here with Jane, getting it all together."

"Is there anything that I can do to help?"

"Sure, you can help with the icing on the cake this year."

"Splendid. That sounds simple enough."

"Yes, it is homemade, and we think that we will have it this evening as a prep for tomorrow. Dinner is just a simple grill and vegetables, as the feast is tomorrow."

"Sounds lovely. Gradey will be here in about twenty minutes; he called me from the car."

"Good news," said Jane as she was preparing the stuffing for the turkey.

"Yes. It has been a lonely week without him," admitted Kascey.

"Glad that you are satisfied now, dear," answered Kelly.

"Yes, it is all done now," chimed in Jane with her friendly advice.

It was so comforting for her to see Kelly and Jane making preparations as usual for the family. There had been so much to plan for the trip, as paperwork and testing were required. She was hoping to see another Thanksgiving with them, and they had basically become the same bubble from the last gathering. The family had been isolating for the special occasion.

Kascey was also conscious as to how she dealt with the two other women in Gradey's life. She took dealing with the women in her husband's life with a grain of salt. Her laid-back upbringing was her training to just cope with it all and to tone it all down in personal situations.

She heard the buzzer as Damian rushed to the door to let his son inside. She could hear the excited expressions as they greeted. It felt as though Thanksgiving had begun.

"Wow, something smells good in here," he said as he poked his head into the kitchen.

"Hello dear," Kelly said as he turned excitedly.

"Hi, Mom, how are you?"

"Wonderful now that you are here safely."

"Good. Jane, how has it been?"

"Just good helping with everything, my son."

"That's good. Kas, how's it going?" he said, turning to her inquisitively.

She rushed over to give him a hug. "So grateful now," she said.

"I know, so grateful. Now I had better freshen up like you said, hon," he replied.

"Yes. I have forgotten." They had discussed the precautions that they would take and were on target.

"Don't worry. I have it under control, and I am fine. See you all in a bit."

He whisked up to his area of the house. A sense of

familiarity radiated from all parts of the house as he climbed the stairs and took in the fresh aroma of washed linens and polished panelling. He tossed his bags in his room, which he inspected as something had changed and he could not figure what. The bed looked bigger, and there was a large sofa. He thought that it must have been nearly impossible to get everything in there. Married life had changed everything, including the familiarity of his childhood bedroom. Once unpacked, he consciously changed his attire.

After his trip, he rushed down again, refreshed and a bit weary, afraid that he had missed something. He still had not seen Lucy and Nate, who were settled in the living room with Maura in front of the television, sipping drinks.

"Hello hello," he said as he stepped in.

"Well, hello. How was your stay?" asked Lucy.

"Splendid. Glad that it is over. Wait, you can't be drinking that," he replied jokingly.

"It is just a mocktail," she replied sarcastically.

"I see. Nate, how has it been?"

"Perfect. Just resting this weekend and looking forward to a wonderful time with my new family."

"Thanks, sounds good. We are glad to have you."

"It is nice to be here," he replied as he rested his hand on Lucy's.

He waved to his aunt, who was nestled in an armchair with blankets. "How are you?"

"Wonderful, dear. I am much better even though it is difficult getting around," she replied as she shifted.

"That is good to hear. We are going to have an awesome weekend as usual."

"Such a joy to spend another year."

"I know, Aunt Maura; I know."

Kascey entered and was relieved by how well Maura looked. She got a chance to embrace Gradey fully as they joined everyone and sat on the sofa in front of the television. It was displaying news of the heightened travel.

"How have you been?" she asked.

"Much better now," he reassured her.

"How did it all go?" she asked.

"It went well and promising. I missed you so much, though. I am glad to be here with you," he whispered.

"Same here, and so happy to have you back. Dinner is almost ready."

"I must confess that I am a bit hungry."

Just then Damian entered, offering more drinks and hors d'oeuvres.

"Let me help you," offered Kascey.

"No, that is all right. No need to worry. We are a small crowd this year."

The family were still feeling the effects of the social distancing. Many were not travelling and would sit this one out. Gradey had not invited any of his college friends, and the town was quiet.

"Son, have you decided what to do about the tech company?"

"Yes. We spent the trip going over the financials, and downsizing is the strongest option."

"You mean unless you can get another investor?"

"No, I mean that I want to increase the share price, and to invest more capital will just be superficial if the ills of the company have not been cured."

"I see. I am willing to add some more as an investment if you need it," he offered.

"Thank you for your concern, and I really appreciate it, but I really do not want to put good money after bad if I do not make a profit. A slimmer engine is what it needs," he answered graciously.

"I see. Regardless, we are here if you need." Damian took a special interest in his son's needs so that he could have the incentive to succeed in business. He had spent a lot of time mentoring him and wanted him to be as successful as he was.

"I appreciate it." They stopped talking so much in front of everyone and focused on the news. Luckily, Nate was in a different industry and had his own corporate issues with which to contend rather than nose around in another's affairs. He would have liked to have thought of himself as more trusted, even though they had known him only one year.

Kelly came out of the kitchen and announced, "Dinner is served."

"Thanks, Mom," answered Gradey, who was followed by Lucy as they gathered around the table.

"It is just really casual tonight. Just help yourselves to the buffet in the kitchen."

"Thank you dear. Maura, no need to worry; I can help with your plate," offered Damian.

"Well, Kascey, we are interested to know how your parents are doing?" Kelly remarked.

"They are fine, thanks. I have not had a chance to speak much since the case."

"Oh, so sorry to hear that. Please send them our kindest regards when you can."

"Thank you. They will appreciate that."

They sat in their seats around the living room, said grace, and commenced their feast as they did every Thanksgiving eve. It was as if they had not missed a beat, and although wounded by the events of the year, they were still having some form of tradition so that they would not write off the year in full. It would not be for another year that they would see the bustling of the city streets and full trains and planes for the holiday seasons. The world would open to bright lights and excitement as in yesteryear, as if the events of the previous year had not happened, with only the remnants of its memory.

"Everyone, we are blessed that we are here again," Kelly stated. "We must think of those who unfortunately are unable to say that: those who do not have a meal tonight, those who are alone, and those in uncertain times."

Damian spoke up. "Sadly, these are tough times for everyone. Where there is loss, we must counter it with the good and try to be optimistic. We have been lucky so far and must be profoundly grateful to see each another. We have seen our Maura make it through illness. We have overcome legal issues with Kascey's designs, Gradey has kept his profession going, and Nate has managed to keep his stores afloat. While our Lucy has the joy of bringing a new member to the family. We could not ask for anything more this year."

"That was beautiful dear," replied Kelly. "Let us give thanks."

"That is right, Dad, and thanks for the delicious dinner," added Gradey.

"Thank you. It is delicious, Mom, Jane."

"Wonderful, dear. I am glad that you enjoyed it."

Jane chimed in. "Thank you. I hoped you would enjoy it. We have been busy all day. I am just so happy to see everyone again." She settled in her chair some distance from anyone. She had become a member of the family, and the children would not feel the holiday spirit without her. She was an honorary family member. She had the meal for the big day organized, as she had done for the last twenty years with the family. As usual, she stayed in a small inn in town and would leave them to a bit of privacy before returning with the feast. She had looked after them for the all the family holidays and visits to the cape, which was her local town. Jane had her own family life, but Gradey's family were like her surrogate family.

"Yes, a wonderful job after all that hard work," Damian complimented them.

"Thank you, dear," answered Kelly. More compliments followed around the table as they cherished the moment of being together finally.

After dinner, they reminisced about past holidays and memories in anticipation of the big day. The family settled in the living room and had a nostalgic session of Thanksgivings past. Kelly shared photos from the album and recalled the good times. It was special, as she saw an inner meaning after the experience of another year. There was a distinct aroma of pumpkin and spices wafting from Jane's traditional pie. She had worked late into the evening baking the pies until it was time to return to the local hotel. She had worked until she ached, as was customary every year. It was her time to shine, and she had been managing the holidays for many years.

Once again, Damian and Kelly were the last to turn in. They switched off the lights and slowly ascended the stairs. "Happy Thanksgiving, and may your dreams come true," he said as he placed his arm around her.

"Thank you, dear. Happy Thanksgiving."

Kascey and Gradey tried to warm up under the crescent moon in his quarters.

"I have a nightcap," he said.

"What?"

Yes. Bristol cream?"

"I don't believe you. Where did you get that?"

"I purchased it in duty-free. Here is a gift for you."

"Thank you. That is so sweet." She opened the package. "This is lovely. A tennis bracelet. You shouldn't have, and thank you."

"I am glad that you like it," he replied proudly. "I knew that you would like it."

"I really do. Not too much, was it?"

"No, not at all," he denied adamantly. "Besides, nothing is too good for you."

"I am so happy. It is perfect," she replied convincingly.

"Fantastic," he said as he leant in for a kiss. "This feels strange."

"Why?" she asked peculiarly.

"Just being here with you in my old room as a married man. I just find it so strange."

"Oh. Well I …" she replied, shocked.

"No. There is nothing wrong. It's perfect. I am cherishing it."

"Really?" she smiled, looking a bit nervous.

"Yes." He laughed.

"Shh," she replied. "Not so loud." They snickered like two college romantics.

They sipped their drinks as he recounted stories from his high school and college years with friends and family in the town. The conversation ran on, and there was no recollection of when they finally drifted to sleep. The sun rose dimly as they awoke to a late and freezing morning.

"Look, it is snowing," he said as he opened the curtains to freshly fallen snow glistening in the morning sun. It had covered the front lawn. "Isn't this beautiful?"

"Yes. It is gorgeous. We should take a walk," she suggested, enchanted by the scenery.

"Want to? I mean, it will be freezing outside," he responded, unconvinced by her suggestion.

"Yes. We should get some of the others to join us. Just for a little bit. When will we get the chance again to have fun in the fresh, crisp outdoors? The holidays in the city will be a little bit different. Unless you count the terrace."

"Right then. A nice walk after dinner. But I do not know about Luce in her condition. She might have to stay with Aunt Maura."

"Do you smell that food? It smells delicious. Should I go downstairs and help?"

"If you want to, but I am sure that they have it all under control. They have been doing it for years."

"Yes, but I do want to show my appreciation."

"Do not worry. They know that you are grateful, and seriously, they have it under control. There is something about that."

"Okay," she answered, sounding a bit discouraged.

"Why don't we freshen up? I have a bit of a headache, but we have to get down there."

"Sure. I am not surprised after last night. How late was that?"

"It was well after midnight," he answered with a smirk.

"Right then. I am going to start." She hopped out of bed and placed her robe over her silk pyjamas.

"I wish that everyday could be like today. Happy Thanksgiving!" he said has he drew her close.

"Happy Thanksgiving, dear," she answered.

~~~~~~

The family were already assembled in the living room and kitchen, preparing. It was past eleven, and Kascey and Gradey sauntered down the stairs to wish everyone a happy holiday. Kelly and Jane were busy in the kitchen as they entered. Jane could hardly lift her head as she greeted them, as she was deep in concentration. Kelly looked up and turned to talk to them.

"My, you two are a bit late getting up this morning," remarked Kelly.

"Yes. We had a bit of a late morning; it has been a hectic week for us both at work," confessed Gradey.

"Sorry about that. If you need any help, just let me know," offered Kascey in conciliation.

"Not to bother, dear. We have it all under control, and thank you," Kelly politely answered with a smile.

"Sure, I understand," Kascey said as she and Gradey exchanged sideward glances.

"Now, lunch will be at one thirty; do have a seat in the sitting room with the others. Oh, and Gradey, can you pass these clean glasses to your father? There are some fresh carrot-and-banana muffins. I have added some cranberries, just how you like them."

Janet then looked up from her conscientious preparations and smiled in agreement. "Yes, we have been over the stove all morning again," she said proudly.

"We can see that," Gradey replied. "Mmm, delicious. Thanks, Mom," he said as he took a few bites. "Here, have some." He offered the muffin to Kascey.

"Thanks," she said as she took a bite and tasted the various flavours. "Wow, these are fabulous. I must get the recipe," she remarked.

"Sure. I will send it to you. They are Gradey's favourite treats around the holidays," answered Kelly.

"Thanks, I would really appreciate that."

The two entered the living room with the items and placed the glasses down. They continued to munch on the warm muffins.

"They smell wonderful," noted Lucy.

"I know. Happy Thanksgiving sis, Nate,"

"Same to you. Thought you might have risen earlier," noted Lucy.

"I know. We have had a tough week and needed some rest. We have the red-eye out tomorrow to get back to the city, so we thought we would take a few moments."

"Sounds good."

"How are you feeling?" asked Kascey.

"I am all right. Psyched that next year we will have an extra person," she said, as she referred to her growing midriff.

"I know. It is really exciting. I am so happy for you," replied Kascey.

"Any chance that you are thinking about having one?" she asked decisively.

"Well, not at the moment," she answered as she glanced at Gradey. "Eventually," she promised.

"Well, that is good," answered Lucy as she glanced at Nate. Just then Maura appeared while Damian guided her to the chair and Gradey went over to assist as she sat.

"Morning, auntie, Happy Thanksgiving!"

"Happy Thanksgiving, dear," she said as she took her seat, appreciatively looking at them.

"How are you this morning?" asked Lucy.

"Very well, dear. Happy Thanksgiving!"

"Happy Thanksgiving, auntie," she replied gratefully.

"May you have many more, and may you have a happy family."

"Thank you, auntie, I appreciate it." Lucy had been the favourite niece all her life. Maura considered her like a daughter. She doted on her and praised all that she accomplished.

"Thank you, Aunt Maura. We are so pleased to see you coming along so well."

"So blessed, dear, to have this behind me."

"Anyone care for some coffee?" offered Damian.

"Yes, please. Why don't I help you?" offered Damian.

"Okay. How many? Two? three? Lucy?"

"No thanks, Dad, just three."

"Sure thing. Coming right up."

Damian and Gradey went to the kitchen to get the drinks.

"So how are you doing?" Damian asked his son.

"Pretty good. We had to rest in a bit. Had a long day yesterday."

"I know. Pace yourself. It is not going anywhere. Any more news about her case?" Damian inquired.

"Yes. They have been charged and should wrap it up by December. Kascey is asking for damages. She has been wrought over the fact that her designs have been duplicated and she was hacked."

"Gosh. Sounds serious. I am so sorry."

"Thanks. We got Norsa, the lawyer, to handle it. She is great, and Kas did not have to worry about a thing."

"Good news, and it sounds promising. I wish you luck. Anything you need, I am always here," he reminded him.

"I know, and I appreciate it, Dad."

"Sugar in the coffee?" he asked as he delicately stirred the mixture to create froth.

"No thanks."

The family assembled in the living room this year for the feast. Once again, as every year, there were many options and courses, with the turkey and all the trimmings laid out as a buffet on the dining table. It was a celebration, and there were moments of prayer and Thanksgiving. Kascey enjoyed being with the group, who had such a joy of family, blessings and happiness, and the little things of which to be grateful. She had her gratitude vignette all practised as they went around the table. She would concentrate on her new life with Gradey, and her previous start-up success with the challenges that had engulfed most of her autumn. She had been married for almost a year and could not be more grateful for the wonderful people in her life.

"I am thankful for my husband," she said as she sweetly turned to him. "Also, having you all in my life. I am new here, and it has been amazingly easy to get to know you all. Thank you for being so supportive of Gradey and me, and for this delicious meal once again, Kelly, Jane, and for the fact that I will be a new aunt. I know that our time will come one day, but now we have something precious to dote on until we get to that point," she said as Gradey looked on admiringly.

"Thank you; that was a lovely statement," admitted Kelly, who had a strong position as matriarch. "Gradey?"

"Well, I second all that she has said," he joked. "However, this year has taught me what family means to me—what it means to have a perfect wife"—he tilted his head towards Kascey—"a wonderful and supportive family, a respectable job, and strong faith to get us through this time." He did not want to go into the harrowing details of what they had witnessed.

"Wonderful, dear, and thank you for sharing that with us. So happy that we could be of help," said Kelly.

Lucy and Nate also showed an appreciation for their pregnancy; and Maura, the success of her operation. The feast went on and was completed with a large dessert of pumpkin pie and other assorted cakes. Jane busily presented the iced ginger cake.

"Here it is," she said as she walked to the buffet table, "— The house-specialty ginger cake."

"Marvellous, thank you," said Kelly as she stepped over to examine it.

"It is gorgeous," remarked Lucinda.

"Thank you. And Kascey iced it. Now I will slice it for you, and you can take whatever you want. Right in the middle is the moistest."

"Well then. Let's dig in," said Damian.

The afternoon was very much the same as on previous Thanksgivings. Kelly was determined to keep the momentum of the tradition alive. It was a toned-down lunch, and the family afterward took a short, brisk walk to burn the calories.

"This is great. I can't wait to get back to the elliptical," Gradey said after a week of unorthodox behaviour from the travel.

"Yes. Definitely after this weekend," replied Kascey. "It is a bit brisk out."

"I know. We usually have some touch football, but I think that this will be a short walk. Good call, though. It has done some good."

"I know. Sorry to have left Maura at the house."

"Not to worry. She is fine with Luce, and believe me, we will all be back inside soon,"

"Race you to the finish," she teased as she took off to warm up.

"I'll get there first," he said as he sprinted.

The snow left a frosty finish on the lawn and on the roof of the Victorian-era wooden house. It was just off the main street, and the tree branches had become spiny and covered with fallen snow. Kascey's outdoor boots had formed a wedge in the snow as she climbed the steps to the front door. She had to take giant steps, raising her knees high to navigate across the path to the entrance.

"I win," she said as she hopped onto the porch.

"I guess. Anyway we are back," he said as he saw Nate and Damian reach the top of the driveway.

"We have more shovelling to do," noted Damian.

"I'll help with that," offered Nate. "It all fell suddenly anyway."

"Thanks, Nate," replied Damian. His new son-in-law was beginning to grow on him. He was passive and hardworking. His job was stable, and he was a decent person. He now saw him as an exceptionally reliable man who had taken his daughter away very quickly. He had forgiven that, as it is to be expected when a couple are in love. Damian now had control of the situation, if only for a few days, and saw that they had a very innate and amicable relationship, which pacified his concerns as a father. There was something about this first holiday season with him that allowed him to, for the first time, feel as though he had truly gained another son, and he could foresee him being in the family for many years.

"Good workout," Gradey said as he entered the living room with his aunt and sister.

"Glad to hear it. Although it is freezing out there," Lucy replied.

"I know, but it was worth it," he answered.

"I couldn't chance it, dear, this time," added Maura.

"I know. Next year, right?"

"Right, dear, next year," she promised.

He rubbed his hands together next to the fireplace and offered some coffee.

"That's all right I will go and make it," he said.

"That was really very thoughtful what you said," Lucy said to Kascey.

"Really, I hoped that you would appreciate it."

"Yes I loved that speech. Anytime that you and Gradey want to get to know my little bundle of joy, just say. We just want to have you both in our child's life as family members, and we are also considering as godparents. There will be a few. I mean, do you remember Trudy from last summer on the cape? Well, summer before last?"

"Yes, I do. How is she?"

"She is well. She moved to Springfield during the pandemic. She is also on the list."

"That is splendid news. We would be honoured."

"Thank you. I am so happy. We have not picked a name. If it is a girl, I like Annabelle; and if it is a boy, Theodore."

"Those are beautiful names."

"Yes. Theodore was my grandfather's name," added Maura.

"Really? I did not know. Anyway it is a lovely name."

"I like Annabelle. I'm hoping for a girl."

"Well let's hope. What does Nate want?" asked Kascey.

"He is not bothered really," she replied as she took a sip of her drink.

"I suppose not," replied Kascey.

The family sat on the sofas in the living room and laughed at what was on the television until late in the evening. Kascey and Gradey had to pack and needed another bag for the care packages that Jane had prepared for them. Kascey had a lovely holiday. She was satisfied that she was able to show her appreciation to her new family. She spent quality time with her husband as if they were college sweethearts, and she was looking forward to her new roles as aunt and godmother. She felt her purpose after the last few months had been oarless for them. She could see a clearer path ahead, and not just for the next few weeks; her mind had opened to seeing the next few years, and there was the possibility of long-term planning again. It had been abruptly taken from them. She felt as though she would be seeing everyone again after the prospect had been so dim just a few months ago. As for her own family still in shielding in Canada, she was now more certain that the holidays would bring promise that she would be able to see them again.

"Are you all right?" asked Gradey as he placed his arm around her.

"Yes, fine. I have just had a long day. It was a perfect holiday."

"It was, and thank you for being here and celebrating with us. I am thankful for you," he answered.

"Me too, and I would not have been anywhere else. I am thankful for you too."

They nestled together and tried to get some rest. There was a long and hectic day back to the city to look forward to, as well as more testing to get back to work. They anticipated a short flight but also increased traffic while going to the apartment on Black Friday. However, there were no anticipated crowds this year, as there had been no parade. Next year was another year to look forward to hopefully; it held the promise of a new normal. The hustle and bustle infused the city while packed trains and flights returned leaving the remnants of the previous year dissipating in the holiday spirit.

The temperature had dropped with the morning's rise. Wrapped in their urban city wear, the couple packed into the car and were driven to the airport to catch their flight to the city. Gradey reassured his mother that they would be seeing each other soon.

"Yes, Mom, do not worry. We will be fine. We will see you at Christmas. Promise."

"Looking forward to it. Have a safe flight, dears," she said as they shut the car door to drive off.

"Thank you," Gradey replied.

"Thanks, Kelly. See you soon, and thank you all for the lovely Thanksgiving," replied Kascey.

"Sure, dear. See you all soon." She waved as the car drove off. Gradey noticed she was always a little reticent to let go after such a wonderful time together. However, he was relieved that she had the rest of the weekend with the family to consider and would manage to compose herself.

"I do not know what gets into Mom; she seems to get a little emotional every time." said Gradey.

"No, she will be fine. You must see it her way. She must let go every time that you leave after having you around again. Must be difficult for a parent."

"You are absolutely right. You have such good intuition." The ride was smooth in the brisk, cool air. It was a sunny day and a perfect day to fly.

"We are lucky that we chose today to fly. There is no telling what the visibility will be like tomorrow."

"I know. We have so much to get back to. At least everyone has slowed down this weekend."

"Right. Things are back to normal for me next week. We have unwelcome news to give at the tech company."

"Really? So sorry to hear that," she replied.

"Yes. It is going to be an ordeal. Probably a bit of bad press as well. There was no real option."

"Oh well. Can you not get them back?"

"Yes, and it is part of the deal."

"Splendid. There is stress from my case too."

"Really? I thought that it was going in the right direction."

"It is, but there is so much paperwork and name-blaming. It is draining. I am so inspired by Norsa's skills. She is so talented."

"I have no idea how she does it too. You have one of the best representations. Take it easy. It will all work out," he reassured her.

"Thank you. Well, I have you."

The car pulled up to the small airport, and they disembarked. The registration and clearance were smooth, as it was still early in the morning.

"I do not mind the extra expense with the low-carbon jet back to the city. There is too much to risk with all of this flying."

"I know what you mean. This is a clever idea," she said as they took their seats in the small charter jet.

"We should be at LaGuardia by one p.m. local time," the steward assured them.

"Thank you," Gradey responded. "It should be a smooth ride, right?"

"Sure thing, and happy holiday," he replied.

"Just enough time to take a little nap," Kascey said as she placed her head on his shoulder.

"Sure. I will just go over some emails."

"Hmm," she said as she closed her eyes.

By the time they arrived, the door attendant greeted them on the way in as he held the door. "Thank you, Raul. How was your Thanksgiving?"

"Happy Holiday to you too. It was good, and thank you. There are a number of residents here this year," he answered.

"Happy holiday, and good to hear," answered Gradey.

"Yes, Raul. Happy Holiday, Thanks," Kascey added.

Kascey was now eager to manage the rest of the weekend in the apartment. She had a modest holiday dinner planned of roasted salmon fillet and sweet potatoes with a coconut cream pie.

"Right, darling," she said. "I have a little dinner planned."

"Really? That was thoughtful of you," he replied.

"Thanks. I just thought that you would want a little change. Or else we can order in some Pinelli's."

"We can do that tomorrow. What have you planned?"

"Salmon and some coconut custard cream pie."

"Sounds good. A little tropical today."

"Yes. A slight change from the ordinary. Do you want some lunch, or shall we just order some sushi, salad, or bagels?"

"Whatever you wish, dear. I will be in the study," he replied.

"Right then. I'll order some salads for lunch."

"Perfect," he replied as he stepped into his office. "I'll only be a few hours," he promised.

"Not to worry. I have the holiday catalogue to go over and orders to fill."

"Good for you," he replied.

She smiled as he closed the door. Back in the apartment, life was back to normal. He had transformed into that worker she had got to know over the summer. The apartment had become a zone for work and not for recreation. She flipped through the menu for the deli across the street to place the order, which arrived in rapid time. She rushed to the kitchen to dish it out for them.

"Grade, do you want yours in the den?" she called from the kitchen.

"I am just in the middle of something dear. Can you leave it on the counter and I will collect it? Thanks."

"Sure." She did not want to press while he was at work. It sounded as if something had come up.

Gradey scrolled through his emails. Roger had rejected a few of the suggestions. It was to be expected, since he was trying to protect the work force. He called Claude immediately.

"Why don't we just give more allowances and benefits to the furloughed staff?" he asked Claude.

"Yes. We can offer that, but we cannot go too high."

"Right then. What did he think of the relocation?"

"He is not going to agree to that," Claude responded despondently.

"Well, we have to convince him. Perhaps a video call on Monday."

"I will try to book it."

"Good. By the way, how did yesterday go? Are you officially getting married?"

"Yes, actually. She said yes."

"Congratulations! That is good news."

"Thank you. I will let you know when we get out of this and can plan a proper celebration."

"Good. Let us know."

He was still in disbelief when he hung up. He collected his salad from the kitchen and joined Kascey on the sofa as he placed it on the coffee table for lunch.

11 | Countdown

Once Monday had arrived after the holiday, Kascey prepared for an early start at the studio to get a head start on the orders. After a brief farewell to her husband, who anticipated a full day of stress from the markets, she headed out the door. On her agenda were meetings with Norsa and more orders to fill. They were piling in for the holidays, which were only a few weeks away. There was a remote prospect of more restrictions hanging over the holiday season. It had been seen in other jurisdictions, and this city was on the watch list. From her experience over the year, she had to remove her mind from the issue and start her day.

After having enjoyed a very reclusive holiday in the city, Syre and Judee were already at the studio, diligently reviewing the orders. Needless to say, it was the most hectic time of the year. Kascey required that her manufacturers work more quickly and entertained the thought of having her family business supply her with the material. Her orders had become more international as buyers were increasingly unable to travel to shop. Since there was word that more restrictions might be looming, it seemed a possible solution.

Once ensconced in her chair and viewing her screen, she said, "We must get these out in time, and they are mounting."

"Yes, we are definitely working on it. We are now on a tight schedule, and the holiday season has started—and the stress is also rising," answered Syre.

"We just got an order in for three of the evening gowns," added Judee.

"That is marvellous. The increasing demand requires another manufacturer on board. How about Mabel?"

"That would be an innovative idea. We definitely need it," said Syre, elated.

"I thought so. I will give them a call. A call is long overdue anyway."

She picked up her phone and called her mother, apparently a bit trepid after not having seen her over the past few months. It was impossible to travel, which would be the case for a few more months.

"Mum. How are you and Dad?" she asked, listening intently to her response.

"We are well. Thank you for asking, and it is such a relief to hear from you, albeit a few weeks before the holidays."

"I know. I am sorry. It has been so hectic with the case and getting the orders out," Kascey explained.

"Not to worry. We still have technology. You sound a bit rushed; is there a problem?" she replied, detecting her daughter's anxiety.

"Well, we need to send some more orders over to you.

We can't fill them quickly enough here, and there are more restrictions."

"That is fine. We just got the Okay to relax restrictions in the suburbs safely, and we can start working on them straight away."

"Good. Thanks, that would be perfect," she replied. She knew that she could rely on them. It was the family business on which she was raised, and she had knowledge of the fabric suppliers and their reliability. Also, when she started her business, she was given the reassurance that they could assist in any way. "I appreciate it," she continued, relieved.

"Now, how are you holding up otherwise?"

"We are fine, I guess. One day at a time. We just had a lovely and quiet Thanksgiving with his folks. It was all safe," she responded before hearing her discord. And now I have the holidays to get through."

"Well, keep up the challenging work. It will all pay off. Remember that."

"I will, Mum," replied Kascey.

"Now, are we going to see you in the keys for New Year's?"

"Certainly, if the travel advisories do not change. It is harder to keep up, as it seems as though they can change so easily."

"Fabulous. We will look forward to that weekend, although your father and I might be stagnated for a while if the advisories change while we are abroad. I suppose that it is the risk that we will take. It is a pity about Christmas, though. It is best to be safe and not travel far. What will you do?"

"We will probably have a quiet one or spend it with his folks at the cape."

"Good. I would plan a private one, as the town now has only a few cases. Who knows … maybe some grandchildren in the future?"

"I really can't say. Look, I have a virtual meeting with the lawyers in a few minutes, so I must go, but thanks, and we will get these orders to you," she replied hastily.

"Sure, dear, and have a wonderful day. I will tell your father that you have called."

"Thank you. Love you all, and can't wait to see you."

"Love you too, dear."

She hung up, smiling at the staff, who seemed to have one ear engaged on the call.

"Good. Let's send some orders that way. She has a lot of fabric in her facility." Memories took Kascey back to being a little girl in the factory and seeing all the swathes of fabric and the contrast of the assorted colours and patterns. It was all that she knew as a child. The aroma of freshly cut fabric emanated throughout the factory, and she could hear the sound of shears as it was cut to size.

"Great. I will do as soon as possible," Judee replied.

She waited to click on the link from Norsa on her computer. Norsa had planned a Zoom call with her assistant to give Kascey an update on the agenda of the case.

"She clicked on the link, and Norsa appeared with her imposing and yet relaxed temperament. Kascey immediately felt at ease.

"Hello, hope you are well," Norsa began.

"Fine, thanks. I love technology."

"Yes. This has been a way of life for most of the year. Now look, we have filed the documents and the cease-and-desist injunction. I can tell you that as of last Friday, there was no trace of the website or your designs. That means that they have complied with the order. I suppose that the damages scared them off."

"Well that is good news, right?"

"Yes. The only thing is that it seems as though they have become untraceable, meaning the subpoena may go unchecked. They might not answer or acknowledge it. So we must impose stricter measures. It is hard to admit to anything, and delay tactics are their defence. We are consulting with the lawyers in the region as to their strategy."

"Really? How long are we looking at?" Kascey asked confusedly.

"Not sure. Over a month. Therefore, we have to revisit this next year. I am sorry, because we hoped that it would be over by then. At least by your next show."

"I hope so. I do not want this to weigh on me any more."

"Yes, we know. We are winning the battle, and the fake line has vanished. I suppose the criminal implications have caused them to hide. From our side, it is easy, but there are now authorities involved in their jurisdiction who are adding more pressure, and therein lies the delay."

"Sounds as if it is getting complicated. What are we going to do?" Kascey asked, her voice growing worried.

"I know, and please do not worry. It is complicated, as they are facing fraud and cyber security charges. Just leave it with us. We have half of our agenda and strategy complete; what is left is the hearing for the damages. You should be compensated for the loss to your business and the stress and anxiety experienced."

"Thank you, and I appreciate it all. It is almost over on our end. This is the final stretch, and it will just take a while to locate them and their assets to put a freeze out."

"Perfect strategy. I am so happy that you thought of it," she replied. She was not that familiar with the legal verbiage and appreciated her explanations in plain English.

"Great. Now, if there is anything else that is worrying you, we now have to get to the drafting and issuance of those documents."

"Thank you, and I'll talk to you soon, I know, when you get that submitted."

"Perfect. We will get back to you in a few days," replied Norsa.

Kascey was pleased that it was a short conversation and was mindful that this was all costing her. Norsa's fees were not on a budget, as she was a high-powered international attorney and she knew her strategy.

Kascey decided to call her husband to lift her spirits.

"Well how is your Monday?" she asked when the call connected.

"Just horrible. It is now going my way today," he answered not conveying any inspiration that she had hoped.

"Oh, I am so sorry."

"Don't worry. How is your day??

"Well … I spoke to Norsa and Mum," she replied.

"Really … any news?" he inquired.

"The site has been taken down, and they cannot find the culprits."

"Really? They must have scared them off. Well, that is good news," he replied.

"Yes. I suppose. It will drag on a bit," she said despondently.

"I see," he replied, sounding disappointed. "How is Mabel?" He changed the subject.

"She is good. They are doing some work for us. I cannot handle this all before the holidays, as there is an increased international demand."

"I see," he replied, becoming a little distracted.

"Yes, and she is looking forward to New Year's," she added enthusiastically.

"We all are. Let us just hope that we can get there with everything changing so quickly. Many people are just cancelling their holiday plans, but we will not have interaction with the public."

"Yes," she replied. "Let's hope that we can stay safe. I know there are so many changes with the requirements and with the demand at work; it is hard to figure out how to ship my different packages."

"Not to fear, there will always be a way," he said, encouraging her.

"Now I have to go. I just thought that I would check in. What time do you think you will be home?"

"It might be a late one. I'm sorry. We have not come to an agreement regarding the takeover."

"Okay, I will put your dinner in the microwave," she said empathetically.

"Thank you."

Gradey hung up knowing that he had a full day ahead of him. He had to determine that since they were not all back at the office and would be scattered in different areas over the holidays, he would be dealing with staff all over. There was the continuous effect of new restrictions which might be looming, as had been the case in other cities and states, and he had to plan accordingly.

He rang Claude. "We really need to get this negotiation rolling if we want the new company survive into the new year," he emphasised.

"This has been the most challenging negotiation that we have done," responded Claude.

"I would not have done this if I had known," he replied regrettably. "I mean, what do they want?"

"I think that they feel as though it will turn around for them."

"It will not—not if it has not happened already. We have given staff support, care packages, alternative buildings, work schemes, our own guarantee. This is unprecedented."

"Right, then I think that another conference call is in order."

"Please book one for five p.m. ET or two p.m. Pacific. We have to get to the bottom of this and close this deal."

"I will schedule an appointment myself," responded Claude. "I have built a good rapport with Dan and will call him directly to sort this out. Hopefully Roger will be available."

"I cannot imagine what type of game that he is playing. We have offered them more than enough."

"I agree, and I will make the appointment." replied Claude uncertainly.

He and Gradey had such a progressive meeting in California the week before and now there was a turnaround. Gradey wondered whether they were being double-crossed and that there was ever any intention to agree to their proposal. He anticipated that more negotiation was needed.

"Hi Dan. I thought that we agreed that this was just the ironing-out stage—that we had smoothed out any issues," Claude said.

"Yes. We have a few more issues of concern."

"Look, Gradey would like a conference call this afternoon. He is becoming concerned."

"Right, we can make the call at about twelve p.m.," he explained. "I have to say that Roger is overly cautious about the state of affairs. It is such a beautiful building. There is no need to just take a swipe. I think that there should be more of a grace period rather than just slashing suddenly. That is all."

"Fine. We will have to see how to finesse it a bit. We will see what we can do."

"Good. I am hoping for a more promising deal that would not put the brand at stake. It would be exceedingly difficult to move addresses. More careful thinking is needed. It is part of our brand," Dan replied.

Claude called Gradey. "We have an appointment set up, but I am still apprehensive."

"Really? How did he sound?" asked Gradey.

"It was not off to a good start. They are against the move, in a nutshell."

"Well if we can come up with a compromise in a few hours, I would like to reconsider."

"I will go over the financials again. Perhaps we have missed something."

Gradey tried to think of what could provide more capital. He rummaged through his brain and thought that employee incentive stock options might be a course. He was reticent as to their ability. However, he might want to pass it by them. In that way, there would be cash and investors.

"I think that we can offer some more stock options for the staff. It is a public company after all," Gradey said.

"Perfect idea," replied Claude. "The main options have remained with the executives, and we can diversify into the mainstream."

"Yes. I hope that they will agree and it is not a case of just trying to hold on to voting power. The next board meeting is not until the end of the year."

"I know. We do not have that long to wait."

"There is so much that they can diversify their portfolio into. New opportunities exist, especially during the pandemic. They can even have a delivery service," continued Gradey.

"I know. We have to really be on point this time."

"Yes. This is too much of an opportunity to pass us by, and we have the funds."

"Great. We can take it from there—a new division that will be a courier service for products."

They intricately set out the proposal and kept their fingers crossed for luck. Gradey felt a surge of anxiety as they waited for the call. When it came, Roger appeared adamant that he was to remain true to form, while Dan appeared more conciliatory.

"I have looked over the full proposal," Roger stated, "and as CEO, there is no way that we can rebrand to that extent. A move would affect our marketability, as we are in an area not far from our colleagues and competitors. It is part of our brand to be in this location, and it is who we are. I started this company, and I have a vision and a mission that have to be respected."

"We understand," advised Gradey, "and we can negotiate another way to infuse capital into the business, but you have to be in agreement to a stock option for the staff—smaller investors who would have a stake in the opportunities and have pride in the company. Also, there is a new division that can take advantage of the current climate. A courier service for necessities. Everyone would agree that this is the best time for it. It is technical and can be a part of services. Advertising is suffering, as most people are going out of business, and here is a way to cater directly to the general public. Once you get into this, anything is possible."

"That is a promising idea," Roger replied. "We can do this and keep the building. It has enough space to install a new division, and we must look at the costs. I mean, to get the tangibles for something like this might be challenging. This is a new mobile division."

"I know," said Gradey. "But you can train existing staff and also independent contractual staff who have their own transport."

"We know, but there is a liability for lost items and road accidents," added Dan.

"We are aware of that, and we can work out the logistics in the package. However, it is a good idea and will add revenue," proposed Claude.

"All right. You send in the proposal and we will see," Roger replied.

"We will have that to you by tomorrow," stated Gradey.

Gradey interpreted a sense of ingratitude from Roger. He had a sense that they were acting as though they were doing him the favour. It was something that he would point out to them once this was settled. However, it showed a company that knew its worth, which was why he had decided to invest in the first place.

"Well, that was better," he said to Claude, relieved.

"That was better. Now are they going to accept it?"

"We will see," Gradey replied.

Gradey later arrived home completely lambasted by events of the day. Kascey had ordered a fabulous meal since she had arrived before him. They dined in and relayed the activity of their days. What was motivating them and kept them rolling to the next idea was the promise of the holidays and a new year. It was safe to say that they were ready to see the end of this one. It was difficult to determine where business would be heading again and whether in the next few weeks they would be working from home.

12 | December Frost

Winter set in with a cool and deep chill, and the countdown to Christmas had started as the stores and streets became festive. Despite the new normal and the harrowing memory of the year, the sentimentality and tranquillity of the season was exemplified by the decorations. The holiday mystique of the city appeared normal, and the concentration of the new normal entwined the sentiment. The evening lights and laughter in the streets brought a sense of positivity. It was certain that the resilience of New York and its visitors embraced the new holiday spirit. The shoppers lined the streets and shivered as they stopped to window shop and think of what could be possible very soon as they thought of ways to make the season bright.

Kascey closed early for a Friday. There was just over a week until Christmas, and it grew dark and festive in the neighbourhood. She expected to drive to the cape on Christmas Eve as well as travel to the keys with her family, and she had more tests scheduled. She had contemplated cancelling, but it was a special trip, and therefore, researched travel precautions. The island was where she and her betrothed had got married a year ago. She would minimally celebrate her first anniversary with her husband and parents. She thought of how just a year ago she was full of nerves and hastily planning her nuptials in the tropics. It was remarkable how the year had changed. Still in deep thought, she climbed into the taxi for the short ride to the apartment.

When she arrived and walked through the front door, she could hear Gradey's voice on the phone. He has been busily closing a deal before year's end. She took off her black faux cashmere coat and broad red scarf and set down her tote bag, which contained all her essentials for the weekend.

"Darling, it is me," she said.

"Hi, I am just finishing up something," Gradey said evasively from his home office.

"Okay," she replied. She was getting used to his behaviour, and a stress buster was needed. He had been dedicated to the settlement for days. "Want to order in tonight?"

"Sure, whatever you wish," he called out, sounding a little bothered. She no longer wanted to distract him.

Kascey perused the menus on her phone and decided on teriyaki again. It was one of their favourites. She walked to the door and peered in. "The teriyaki should be here in thirty minutes," she answered.

"Good, and thanks. Sorry, I am just trying to close this. We are almost done."

"Fabulous," she answered. "Although I truly understand your commitment, I have had about enough of it."

"I am sorry. We will have this finalised, and you won't

have to hear any more until the New Year. I promise you," he explained.

"I hope so." she closed the door and sat on the sofa. She was disappointed that this was the outcome of her anticipated romantic Friday night. Her phone beeped; the courier was right around the corner. She watched as the dots slowly moved towards the building. She was stuck with an evening of wrapping the online purchased gifts for the family while her husband was in the study. She flicked through the TV app and saw that there were holiday shows all evening. Feeling that her best option was to return to work and finish the orders, she settled on the settee in front of her computer.

~~~

Saturday brought about a brisk chill as she and Gradey ventured out to find the perfect tree. The strong pine scent swelled in the air as they drew closer to the tree stand a few blocks away.

"Not a large one this year. We really only have a week to enjoy it. We should be back by the fourth," she stated.

"Right. I like this pine here," he said as he picked out a rather robust tree. The aroma filled the sidewalks.

"I like that. How about this one here?" she suggested.

"Sure, that is fine. It is a little taller; I suppose that we can carry it if you take one end and I the other."

There were resonant sounds of the festive season. The Salvation Army was out in full display along the city streets as parents rushed along with children bundled in bright scarves to see the window displays. The outlook for the new year remained optimistic, and people were resilient in keeping their spirits up and to make the most of the season. The smell of chestnuts arose from the few vendors who could operate, as well as cinnamon from the bakery across the street.

"It is getting chilly; we should head back," she commented.

"Right, you grab that end, and I will get this one." He picked up almost the whole tree with warm mittens and laid it down. They stooped to raise it and amusedly walked the block home.

At the door, Raul assisted with the tree while Kascey unwrapped her scarf and removed her coat in the elevator.

"See you upstairs!" Gradey called.

"Sure," Kascey replied, sounding relieved. Once the stress of choosing the right one was over, she focused on the creative part of dressing the tree. She had set out her favourite silver and magenta decorations, as well as white lights and silver ribbons. They set the tree in the stand as she created a very modern twist to a traditional pine tree. Gradey admiringly lingered around as he held the decorations for her to place on the tree.

"You have such talent. Look how you are placing everything in line," he said, looking at her admiringly.

"Thank you. I will place the ribbons on last, maybe spray a bit of frost, and the silver angel goes on the top."

"Wait; let me hold the ladder so it does not fall over, and let me do that," he cautioned.

"Thank you, hon," she said as she steadied herself, "Where is the silk skirt for the stem of the tree?"

"It must be in that box there."

"This is such a tradition," she said. "The holidays were always so special, and then we had New Year's on the island. My family would fly in from Quebec. I miss them so much this year."

"I know. Next year will be different. We will have a lovely holiday with them in Canada, just like when you were younger."

"Thank you. I hope next year will be better times. It has been so trying. We have not seen the end of the situation and the legal case that is going on."

"Sorry, dear. Next year will be better; let's hope."

"I mean, I have been living all over the world, but I always spent this time of the year with them."

"I totally understand. Don't worry; it will get better," he said empathetically.

"Well, on a brighter note then, I think that I will do some baking tomorrow. The spiced ginger cake that you like."

"Splendid. However, tomorrow is a workday for me. I know that it is Sunday, but we are close to finalizing, and the board meeting is in two weeks."

"All right. I understand." Trying to cast aside the fact that she had been making the compromises recently, they continued until the tree was complete. That accomplished, they remained in awe to gaze and marvel at the tree while they sipped espresso in the dark while finally feeling the full holiday spirit. It was their first one in the new apartment, and they wanted it to be memorable.

"Now it feels like the holidays," she remarked. "This year

is so much different than last year," she noted. "This time last year, we were preparing for the wedding and celebrating the holidays with your folks. My new line was just starting."

"Talk about a difference," he said. "And there was no way of foreseeing all of this. One thing about the holidays, they bring hope. I really could not have gotten through it all without you."

"Thank you. I could not have gotten through it without you either," she agreed, sounding smitten.

With the stress of the week behind them, they spent the evening curled up on the couch, making new memories of the holidays in their new co-op apartment under their newly decorated tree. It was the first time that something so magical was in the living room, and a first for them to experience in their new home.

The big day had arrived. Kascey excitedly sneaked to the base of the tree to see what Gradey had placed under it the night before. It was in a small box, and there was another flat box. She figured out that one was jewellery and the other must be something technological. Buzzing with anticipation, she decided to unwrap it while he was still asleep, just before he awoke. They decided to safely drive to the cape in an hour to make a 2.00 p.m. lunch. Traffic was usually clear on Christmas Day along the I-95, and they were prepared for state health stops.

Kascey slid her finger along the side of the wrapping and

pulled it up on one side. She slipped out the box. It was special for their first holiday and was from Tiffany's. She smiled snugly. In admiration, she pulled out a white gold charm necklace. There were a few charms on the necklace already. She held it up in awe. It was just what she wanted. She heard a slight shuffle and put it back in the box.

"Morning, dear. Merry Christmas," he said as he appeared a little dishevelled in his robe.

"Merry Christmas. I was just rearranging the gifts I bought you," she answered mischievously.

"Good. Do you want to open them now or after some coffee or something?"

"Let's do it now," she said unreservedly.

"Right. Wait, these are for you," he said as he handed them to her.

"Thank you. Look, a nice small box!" she exclaimed. "Here are your gifts, dear."

"Thank you. Wow, you sure went all out," he noted.

"Yes. All necessary," she replied.

"Good, then you go first," he offered as she began to rip off the paper of the small box.

"Thanks. Oh, it is so perfect," she replied as she lifted the necklace from the box. "I love it, and thank you. I have always wanted one of these."

"I am glad that you like it. It was such a hard choice this year."

"Wonderful. And what is this?"

"Wait and see," he replied.

She tore open the paper and looked at the box. "A new tablet and phone. They are beautiful, and you know that I really need these with all that I have to do now. Thank you."

"Yes, and you are welcome. I am glad that you like them. They are the new line from that tech company."

"I see. Well, they are perfect. Marvellous. I can't wait to get connected."

"They should have a built-in signal for those weekends in the Catskills."

"Oh, great, you thought of everything. Now open your presents," she said anticipatingly.

"Thanks. These look great." The wrapping was very decorative and stylish. "I don't want to spoil it," he said as he ripped open the paper. "Wow, an outdoor survival kit. That is fabulous. Just what I need for our weekends. I love it. And there is another one."

"Yes, just a few more things that you will need."

"Great, thanks. I love these shirts and this wool scarf. These are the best. I can wear this on our drive today."

"Yes, it should keep you warm," she said proudly as he wrapped it around his neck.

"Now we had better get a move on and have breakfast. I have some cinnamon rolls and smoothies in the kitchen. Shall I get some coffee?"

"Wait a minute, dear. I will get the coffee and the rolls. It is Christmas, so take a break."

"Thank you, dear," she replied as she relished his pampering.

On the holiday, and now through the year, it was customary for them to donate to the food charity downtown. Kascey had readied the items she had purchased for those who were to have a very deprived holiday season. There were still long lines to the food banks, and she was concerned to see it all. She wanted assist those who were suffering in any way possible. It was a global issue for them, and she wanted to start at her home. They had donated to the college fund for the underprivileged in the city and had sought to act as mentors. Among the holiday spirit, there were still those in need. They had donated their time and options to their mentees who were inspired by them and wanted to enter the field.

~~~~~~

By 10.00 a.m., they were packing the four-wheel drive with the gifts for the family. "Now I have gifts for Lucy, Nate, your parents, Aunt Maura, Nancy, and that should be it." Kascey counted them.

"Yes. That is it, although Lucy and Nate have opted out this year. We had better leave in time for the lunch. Right. Do we have our test results and the certificates again?"

"Yes we do. Right then, I will just hop in," she placed her plum patent leather pump on the ledge and raised herself up. She wrapped her grey wool pencil skirt and grey coat in as she sat upright. She had on a wine sweater and matching gloves. She wore a small fedora with her brunette hair just beneath the nape of her neck, and a black wool scarf.

"You look really fixed up. They will love your attire. My mom and Lucy always admire the way that you dress."

"Thank you, dear." She was in her glory. She was to spend four hours driving with him along the coast. It was a clear December day, and they anticipated a smooth drive. There was snow due by the weekend, she hoped they would be back to the city before then.

"When is our flight to the keys?" he asked.

"It is at nine fifty-five a.m. on the thirtieth. It is actually a charter for safety reasons, but we still have to get tested again a few days before."

"That trip should be a saviour, and my board meeting will be over by then."

"I am looking forward to a long-awaited break," she added.

"Me too."

"How are your parents?" he asked.

"Just fine. That reminds me … let me call them and wish them a Merry Christmas now," she said.

"Right then. I will just concentrate on the road." He steadily drove as they were almost halfway to *Silent Manor*. It was a drive that he made occasionally, and he revelled in the familiarity of going home.

"Hello, Mum, Merry Christmas," Kascey said as Mabel answered her phone.

"Merry Christmas, dear. Ethan, Kascey is on the phone." She called over to her husband who was arranging glasses for the lunch.

"Hi Kascey, Merry Christmas!" he shouted in the background.

"Merry Christmas, Dad. Who have you coming over today?"

"We have the neighbours and your cousins, Martha, and Hamish. One of the neighbours lost his son to the disease, and they are missing him very much today."

"So sorry to hear that. It must be so difficult for them. Anyway, please send them my love and wish them a happy holiday."

"Will do, dear," answered Mabel, "So are you two off to the cape?" she asked with a hint of rejection.

"Yes we are. We decided to do it after all." Kascey detected her mother's tone.

"Good, and have an enjoyable time. Send my love to them all for me."

"Thanks, Mabel, and Merry Christmas!" Gradey interjected in the background.

"Well, Merry Christmas," she replied.

"Thanks, Mum Gradey's a bit brief as he is behind the wheel. I will call you later or tomorrow to see how it all went," Kascey explained.

"Thank you, dear. We will expect your call."

"Have a nice day!" Kascey said.

"Thank you, and you too. Enjoy your lunch, and send my best to Kelly and Damian."

"I will. Talk you to you soon," said Kascey as she disconnected. "Well, they all sound in good spirits," she said, sounding relieved as she hung up. She was a bit despondent about not having been able to see them for months.

"That's great news. I know it is hard not seeing them today; however, very soon we will be in warm weather and bringing in the New Year on an island," he said, consoling her.

"Sounds perfect. I am definitely counting the days. That being said, I am looking forward to lunch at the manor house with your family, dear."

"So am I. Mum and Dad are expecting us in two hours."

"Right then. What do you want to listen to?"

"Mm Michael Bublé?"

"Yes, I love that holiday album."

"Perfect. You can switch that on." He nodded. They were able to enjoy the quality time together and the smooth ride to the cape. They drove along the coast until they came to the sleepy village that had now been eclipsed by the winter's freeze.

"We are getting closer," he commented as Kascey raised her head from the neck of the seat. "Were you having a nap?"

"No, no. I just closed my eyes for a few minutes."

"Not a problem, then; we are here." He pulled up to the house, which was decorated with lights and a holiday wreath. They noticed Nancy's car there.

"Good. The house looks lovely. I can smell food from here," Kascey commented as she opened the car door to step out.

"Yes, it certainly does smell delicious." There was the aroma of ginger and cinnamon and candied yams, as well as a roast. "Now remember, even though we have all been tested, you can decide whether to wear a mask for safety," he advised.

"Thanks darling," she replied agreeing with him.

Kascey had a matching one for her outfit, while Gradey had a navy-and-bronze patterned one. "I am actually looking forward to this fashion accessory," said Kascey.

They gathered the gifts and noticed that there was a distinct chill from the ocean's breeze.

"Yes, I know." Gradey smirked as he accepted the new norm. They stepped inside the foyer bundled with their gifts and could see that the house had been decorated exquisitely throughout. Kelly had a very keen eye for every detail. Damian was carving the roast while Jane and Kelly were adding the final changes to the table.

"Hello everyone!" Gradey called. "Merry Christmas!"

"Merry Christmas, dears," Kelly replied. "So glad that you have arrived just in time. How was your drive?"

"It was great, thanks," he replied. "Dad, Jane," he said, addressing them to wish them holiday cheer.

"Hello, Gradey, Kas. Merry Christmas," he said.

"Same to you, Dad," Gradey replied.

"Yes same to you. Merry Christmas!" replied Kascey. "We were so looking forward to today and have some gifts for everyone."

"Thank you, and Merry Christmas. You can place those under the tree for when it is time," asserted Kelly.

"Great." Kascey walked through to see Gradey's cousin Nancy, who had been isolating for the occasion. "Hello,

Merry Christmas," she said as she placed the gifts beneath the sparking traditionally decorated tree.

"Yes, Merry Christmas," replied Nancy.

"Thank you, and how has it been to be back?"

"These past few weeks have been fabulous. Luckily we had pleasant weather this year," replied Nancy.

"That is good," replied Kascey.

"Good for you. Nice to see you again, and Merry Christmas," Gradey said as they took a seat and continued the conversation.

"Come on in now, dinner is served!" called Kelly.

"Thanks, Mom," they replied as they sauntered to the buffet table that was fully dressed with a lace table runner and red-and-gold crystal decorations. It had a rustic appearance, with pinecones and pine leaves, along with crystal wine glasses.

"It all smells delicious," noted Gradey.

"Yes, as always," said Damian.

"Yes, as always," chimed Nancy. "Look at the delicious vegetables. They must have been fresh from the garden."

The smell of cinnamon, baked yams, gravy, and stuffing with thyme permeated the room. Jane had made fresh baked rolls and iced Christmas cakes for dessert.

They said grace to give thanks for the meal and that they still had each other while they thought about those not present or were missing a loved one. Although a small crowd, they appreciatively tucked into the meal that had been so arduously prepared. Because of the events in the world, Kelly wanted to make the memory incredibly special since they were uncertain when they would have the chance to all be together again. Jane and Kelly left none of their favourite holiday treats out as the family savoured the fruits of their twenty-four-hour labour.

"Once again, my compliments to the chefs," Damian said.

"Thank you, dear, would you like some cranberry sauce? It is homemade."

"Yes, this is wonderful," he said, barely lifting his head as he continued with the items on the plate in front of him.

Gradey continued with his compliment. "Yes, this is absolutely delicious. As always."

"Thank you. Now here are some brussels sprouts," she replied, indicating to him the silver platter.

"Thanks."

"I would not miss this for the world, and I return every year for this delicious meal," Nancy said.

"You are welcome. We are happy to see you," replied Kelly.

"Yes, I love these meals, and I must get the recipe for the stuffing," added Kascey. She envisioned how she would plan her holidays with her family.

"Thank you, Kascey. I will have to give you the recipe someday."

"So, Nancy, what new novel are you working on?" asked Damian.

"I am working on a mystery at the vicarage," she answered.

"Well that sounds very interesting, and if it is anything like your last book, I am sure that it will be a bestseller," he replied.

"Thank you. This one is a little different and not as

thrilling, and is more historical fiction. I thought that I would try that out."

The afternoon turned to evening as they all sat in the living room, distanced, and devoured the dessert and had more laughs. It turned out to be a typical holiday, and everyone was satisfied. They opened their gifts and listened to carols as each slowly retired for the evening. Kascey and Gradey were to make an early start back to Manhattan and needed their rest after a long day.

They looked at the stars from the guest house's window and noted the magical way the frothy waves crashed on the shore below. The moon set a glow on the water and horizon.

"When I was younger, I would count the stars and think of the three wise men," she said.

"Really?" he asked.

"Yes, I would think that they were in the stars and were still bearing gifts."

"That is really special. I used to think of the ships from that carol," he admitted.

"Right. So did I. That is so strange."

"Yes. I would think of the ships coming in from the outskirts of the sea," added Gradey.

"Amazing, and such a vivid imagination."

"Have you enjoyed your day?" asked Gradey.

Kascey glanced at him. "Yes, totally. There is no place that I would rather be."

"You are such a part of us and it all now. I could not imagine it with anyone else."

"Thank you, and that means so much to hear."

They listened to the ocean all evening until the monotonous tone set them asleep.

———————

The morning sun rose to a dull point in the heart of winter; they could not tell what time it was, as it was so dark. Gradey had memories of Boxing Day with his new toys and still being excited the day after. He would rush down and play with them, whether he had received an electronic train set or video games. He yearned for the patter of little feet a more fulfilled holiday by the next year. He wanted children so he could give them the life that he'd had.

"Morning," Kascey said as she opened her eyes. "What time is it?" she looked around sharply.

"It is about ten a.m.," Gradey answered.

"Really? Oh no. I wanted to help with the breakfast before we left," she said sadly.

"Not to worry. They will understand. We overslept," Gradey explained.

There was a distinct aroma coming from the kitchen of baked pumpkin-and-cranberry muffins. They were Kelly's favourite.

"Mmm, something smells good," she noted.

"Yes. I will go and bring some coffee and muffins back. Wait right here," he lightly demanded. He went downstairs as she rushed to shower and get dressed quickly. She was ready in a few minutes. He was confident that she would show considerate guest behaviour.

He returned with the tray of breakfast. "Wow, that was fast," he noted. "Here, dear, all set on a silver tray for us," he joked.

"Thanks. I cannot believe that you let me sleep in," she chided.

"It was not a very long lie-in; besides, we have a long drive back, and you need your rest," he explained.

"Okay that is all right." She succumbed to his innocent face. It was hard to be mad at his charming good looks for long. She walked over to the bed and picked up a muffin.

"These are good," she said with her mouth full as she bit in.

"Yes. They are. There are not that many people up. It was just Mom and Nancy.

"All right, you are forgiven."

"Besides, we really need to head back before the storm, and I have to get some work done for the virtual board meeting on Monday. We will not be travelling, thankfully. It will all be by Zoom. Also we have tests and forms for the new year to prepare."

"Right. I will collect my things in a bit then. I just loved that quilted sofa throw from your mother. It so fits our décor."

"Yes. It was wonderful," Gradey observed. "She loved that gift as well."

"I know. I thought that she could use those appliances since she does so much baking," replied Kascey.

"It was so thoughtful. I am sure that she appreciated it."

"I am glad," Kascey answered. They turned on the news. There was a mixed sentiment that people had observed the holidays all over the world in their own distinct ways. Some were suffering and lonely, and some were together. They replayed clips of midnight Mass and of the Christmas Day bells ringing throughout the world from city to city.

"All right. I will take the bags to the car; we have another half hour before we leave," he said as he looked at the navigator on his phone. The red line back on the expressway was highlighted to four hours and six minutes in good traffic.

They were specific in thanking his parents for a special and private Christmas, as they were uncertain when another similar one would occur. Usually there would be a lunch in town, but there was still distancing for the vulnerable to consider, and the family had opted to spend the holiday in private. Gradey and Kascey donned their masks as they bade farewell and entered the car for the drive home.

Oak and cedar trees lined the roads as they drove along the scenic route back to the city. It was still bursting with the holiday spirit as the frost started to gather on the windows.

Soon the tower blocks of the city were within vehicular reach. In half an hour, they rolled to the entrance to their building. Raul stood and waited for the car to approach to open the door for Kascey as she left the car and Gradey drove to park.

"Thanks, and happy holidays, Raul," she said as she exited.

"Thank you, Mrs. C. And the same to you. Glad that you are back to beat the snowstorm."

"Yes, and just, luckily. Thanks again."

She waited for Gradey to return, and they entered the elevator together. The ride up was silent as they struggled with the new throw and the set of crystal glasses sent from Lucy and Nate.

"It is so freezing that I could really get under this throw now. It is going on the sofa," insisted Kascey.

"Yes, it is warm," Gradey said.

The elevator buzzed as the doors opened on their floor.

"This is us," he said as they exited to their door.

"Home sweet home," Kascey replied as she dropped her bag on the floor. They positioned the quilt on the sofa and turned on the splendour of the tree lights.

"Shall I get some coffee for you with some cinnamon?" he offered.

"Yes please." Kascey curled up on the sofa and felt the warmth of the tightly knitted fabric.

Gradey went to the kitchen to start the brew while Kascey checked her messages. It was a major holiday in Canada. She had yet to phone her family back but would see them in a few days. Work was mounting, and the orders for the holidays around the world were increasing as she checked her sales and output reports.

There were many orders for New Year's coming in as well, some to other parts of the world, and she needed to get on her distributors for express deliveries.

"Thank you, dear," she said as he placed the mugs on the coffee table.

"You are welcome." They spent the best part of the day curled up and watching holiday shows: *Elf*, *The Holiday*, and the more traditional *Christmas in Connecticut*. The news broadcasted the muted holiday spirit in some parts of the world as the city revived from the holiday. They allowed one more day of relaxation as the rest of the world turned around them.

13 | The End of the Year

Monday was frenzied as they prepared for the rush to achieve their agenda as planned by the new year. Kascey had a long day at the office to produce new evening dress orders that were expected before New Year's Eve. The appreciation for expedited shipping could not come at a more opportune time. The staff hurried to fulfil the orders to satisfy all clientele worldwide.

Gradey meticulously prepared for his board meeting and left no stone unturned in the event of a change of plan. The purpose of the meeting was to allow him to certify his position and present his proposals in the memorandum of agreement. The director's meeting was timely and virtual due to travel convenience.

In attendance were Dan; Roger; Malcome, the chair of the board; Gradey; the treasurer; and the officers. The object was to pass the new memorandum and welcome Gradey to the fold as a director and major shareholder. It was unfortunate that this was occurring at a tense time. The situation arising from the pandemic was taking its toll, and the company had to be restructured to survive even though there were profitable essential and tech businesses elsewhere. The distribution was not necessarily part of revenue in certain circumstances. The plan was to increase the revenue and drive up the share price, and many of the members agreed that doing so was in the best interests of the company.

Once they had confirmed the attendance, it was time for Gradey to speak.

"Hello, it is a pleasure to finally meet you all. I understand that we need to vote on the proposals outlined in section twenty of the memorandum. I wholly support the amendments to the mission statement."

"It is a pleasure on our part as well, and we are excited to have you on board," replied Malcome. "Now it is time to count the vote; all in favour, raise your hands." To that, more than 50 per cent raised their hands.

Gradey felt a surge of accomplishment, although the outcome could have been better. Malcome continued. "To the amendment of section twenty-one in the memorandum, all who agree raise your hand."

To that there was a 53 per cent agreement, as Roger did not raise his hand. It was still not a necessity to downsize the canteen.

Gradey was left disappointed that Roger showed such disregard for the proposal. They continued to vote in the proposals and amendments and finally adjourned the meeting. He felt a sense of accomplishment. More creative and ingenious ways to avoid travel were now being used, and Gradey could spend the rest of the week at the office in New York, sorting out the newest project and the plans for the weekend. He was appreciative nonetheless that his objectives had been considered.

"Thank you all for implementing the amendments. It will be a pleasure to do business with you," said Gradey.

"We really appreciate having you on board and wish you luck with the proposals for the sake of the company," stated Malcome. "Before I forget, have a happy New Year, and we will see everyone bright and fresh to get started on the new proposals on January fourth."

Grady disconnected and looked out on the cold, dark December day. It was the end of the year, and the boats were mooring on the river. It was now afternoon, and they were preparing to take passengers to Long Island. The effervescent lights began to guide the vehicles home again, providing a familiar form of normalcy. It was a mystical time of the year, and hope and inspiration still exuded from the notion of a new year.

Kascey was experiencing a long day in the studio, and her staff were working overtime. Some were working remotely. Results of the orders showed that the classic evening gown worn by Moda at the shows was a hit especially in the southern regions and the Caribbean. The orders had mounted the previous week and they were busy meeting the demand.

"Can we get more from the distributor? If not, I will call Mabel for backup," stated Kascey.

"I think that we only have about fifty left in stock. That might be a particularly clever idea," said Judee.

"Perfect. I will do, even if I have to sew myself. We cannot let these people down."

Syre was frantically packing the boxes for the express mail as the deadline for next-day delivery was fast approaching.

Kascey had hired a few interns for the holidays, and the studio was socially distanced, with workers and holiday attire on each counter. She had to put the stress on Mabel, even though they had a fabulous weekend planned in the keys. They rummaged to find enough packing paper to delicately load the dresses in the boxes.

"Thank you, and now we have to print the labels," stated Syre.

There was no room to fit all the boxes before the delivery truck arrived. The studio was stacked with them as staff navigated around them.

"I think that we will have to take a few of the orders to the depot ourselves, because it might be too late to wait until they arrive," noted Kascey.

"Right then, Marisol and Niquita, let's take what we can to the depot," instructed Syre, who was weighed down with most of the parcels. It was a tough job, but someone had to do it. The ladies rushed to place parcels in large bags and on their trolleys to push them to the depot two blocks away.

"Don't forget your coats; it is cold out there!" called Kascey.

It was always a rush around the holidays. But Kascey relished the energy and the excitement of the sales. It was uncertain where the customers would be wearing the dresses this year. There were many private home parties, and the dresses were being shipped to people in South America and the Caribbean, where private resorts had opened. Some were being sent as far as Europe, where there were enough private venues and events taking place, although on a smaller scale. By the time as 6.00 p.m. had arrived, the floors and counters were empty. Kascey had to spend the rest of the evening sewing a few more dresses and had to take her work home.

"Wonderful job today, everyone," Kascey said. "We will have to repeat this tomorrow, as I see a few more orders coming in. We also must think about the week of New Year's Day, which is a season for events. As you know, a number of people consider the holidays to end on Epiphany, and there will be outings and services until then. The market in the Caribbean and some of South America is a religious niche, and the clients wear dressy suits to church and banquets."

Kascey ascended in the lift to her apartment after one of the longest days of the year. Gradey was already settled on the settee, and she turned to him in shock.

"Why ... you are home before me today," she stated.

"Yes, we finalized the deal, and I thought that I would take a little time out. Mind you, it is still afternoon Pacific time."

"I see," she replied with a smile. "Glad to hear it. Well, my evening is not going to be that straightforward. We are inundated with international orders for the rest of the season, and I am going to have to set up here to get a few last-minute items done. Sorry."

"I understand. Look, you have been so understanding these last few weeks and through the holidays, so I will relocate to the bedroom, and you can have this area—unless you want to go to the study?"

"No, but that would be great. I am fine right here. Thanks, dear."

"Not a problem. I suppose I should order something in for us then?"

"Yes, please. that would be amazing." They were still in a quasi-restriction stage regarding the pandemic, and they still had delivery service set up although a smooth transition had been made from how life had been during autumn.

"What would you like to order?"

"Anything would be fine. I am not fussy tonight," she replied. "I do not really have much appetite."

She freshened up and took out her designs and set up her sewing machine and got to work.

"Wow. I see that the hectic season has really afforded a Kascey Couture original."

She smirked. "It sure has. And handmade."

"An original. Right, I will get this all sorted while you work. See you in a bit." With that, he set off to the widescreen TV in the bedroom.

The hustle and bustle on Kascey's agenda made for a sweeping week timewise. It was disjointed, as there were various aspects that had to be tied up before the year's end and people were not due back to work until the first week of January. By Thursday, the couple had gone through what seemed like an eternity since Christmas with all the current events and busy workload. Kascey yearned for a few days away with her family at that point and recalled previous trips to prepare. She was leaving the business in safe hands with the staff, who were working overtime for New Year's Eve. There was nothing that she couldn't really do from a different location from a managerial point of view, and she would take her travel-size sewing machine to assist remotely with any last-minute surprises or delays on return to the city.

She busily packed and planned for the weekend. Based on her experience on previous visits, she packed her customary sarong and pashmina, as well as her swimsuit and sunblock. The list also included a large-brimmed straw hat, insect repellent, masks, disinfectant spray, and a first aid kit. She also brought her makeup, a white blazer, light sweaters, her red New Year's Eve gown, and a pair of festive strappy sandals. She also remembered her protein bars, mini sewing machine, iPad, headsets, *The Beach house* novel, and her exercise kit for romantic jogs on the beach with Gradey. Since she had spent her holidays on the islands as a child each year with her parents, she felt as though she was travelling to a familiar area. They had a villa rented near the beach, while her parents were staying in a suite at the resort. It was a short walk between the two, and Kascey anticipated much interaction over the holiday weekend.

"Gradey, are you packed?" she asked from the bedroom.

"Yes, dear," he replied with bated breath.

"Are you sure? There is not much in your bag?"

"Yes … I am going to do it soon. I am just signing a few documents before we head out."

"Well, the flight is at nine, and it is now almost eight p.m." She reminded him.

"Thanks, dear. Will do. There is not that much."

"Well, you need your tuxedo for the private New Year's function. And then a pair of jeans and a jacket. Do you know what? I will select a few things, and you decide."

"Thanks, I appreciate it. I just have to get this done. It is only five p.m. Pacific, and tomorrow is the day before New Year's Eve, which is the last day to get this out, dear."

"Not to worry; I said that I would do it," Kascey replied sarcastically.

"Thanks," Gradey said, treading lightly. "I am sorry, but I need to have all this work done by the weekend." He was looking forward to the new year, when things would settle for him. There was nothing that he liked about the existing year, and two more days of it would be excruciating.

The evening was a quiet one for them as it waned, and they were about to enter a new geographical zone away from everything. Kascey could sense change and was beyond excitement as she finished the packing and sorting out more orders online.

"We need to break out the champagne early, dear," Gradey said as he walked into the room grinning. "We have finally signed off on the deal, and it is behind us. I am just excited for the weekend."

"Really? That is perfect news. I have it all done; I will get the glasses."

"That's all right. You wait here a second, and I will get them." He walked straight to the cupboard and pulled out the New Year's champagne that they had been saving for the following weekend.

"Here you are, dear. I thought that we would make an early start." They clinked their flutes and toasted to a better year.

The time passed after that, and 9.00 p.m. arrived quickly as they set to bed to catch the early flight to the island. Exhausted from a hectic day, they fell into a deep slumber until they heard the alarm at 6.00 a.m.

"Wow," he said as he turned to check the time. "It is time to make a move." He clambered out of bed and stretched.

Kascey awakened, rubbed her face to get more energy, and climbed out. "It's time to go. We have to get there soon. What time is the car coming?" she asked in very scripted fashion.

"Seven I think," he responded.

"Good. We still have an hour, and it should be twenty minutes to LaGuardia, so we have time. It's a charter, so there aren't any long lines."

"Perfect, darling. Coffee? I'll get some."

"Thanks. I am just going to check the overnight for documents."

She searched through her overnight, where she had everything organized, including their COVID test results.

"Here we are. Some breakfast." Gradey arrived with the tray of coffee and croissants.

"Thank you. Perfect." She took a sip from her mug, "Can't believe that I am seeing my folks for the first time in a year."

"I know. How does it feel? In a few hours, we will be miles away with an ocean view."

"I can't wait. I am super excited. Super excited."

"Great, me too," he agreed. "I feel so relieved, like a heavy weight had been lifted."

"I know. I still have so much to do, but this is so important. I am not sure when I will see them after this, so this really has to matter."

"I know it does. I really do."

They swiftly left and arrived at the airport, where they boarded and settled on the plane. They buckled up and were offered refreshments. It was a three-hour flight along a familiar route as Kascey peered through the window. The small jet followed the jetstream to the southeast coast. The plane landed to a beautiful day, and they were driven to the villa by the sea. It was hidden in an excluded area on the beach and was a beautifully decorated two-bedroom villa. Kascey checked to see whether her parents had landed.

"Hello, Kascey," she heard Mabel say on the phone.

"Mum, are you here? How are you?"

"Yes, we are here. We are just settling in the room, and your father is tipping the porter outside. When did you arrive?"

"We just arrived and must have missed you at the airport."

"I know, but we came commercial direct. How was your flight?"

"It was just wonderful. Smooth and calm. Oh, and Gradey says hello. We are here waiting to see you when you are ready."

"Good. We were thinking about a late lunch downstairs. It is an open restaurant by the pool and should be only a short walk for you," suggested Mabel. She was conscious about the pandemic although they had received their first jab of the vaccine.

"Perfect. We will see you there at about two o'clock?"

"That sounds wonderful. Now Taney was just emailing about one of your orders and wants you to call her. She wants to ensure a cut on it."

"Right, I will do," Kascey was diligent. "I know that this is an important Saturday, and I'm relieved that we can get some things done here."

"Well, that is the issue now. See you later."

Kascey was overjoyed. The emotions took control as she realised that the moment was finally here and she would be seeing them.

"Hey, what is the matter?" Gradey asked as he placed his arm around her.

"Oh, it is nothing. I am fine now." Kascey wiped a tear from her eye. "Tears of joy."

"Fine," he said as he tried to console her. "It's all right. Just look at this lovely place. It is all ours for the weekend. Do you want to take a stroll out on the beach? It is still over an hour until lunch."

"Perfect. I would love that. I need my shawl. It is a bit breezy out," she said as she gathered her comfortable wrap and headed to the door. She was accustomed to the beach and the weather of that time of the year. It was only just a year prior that they'd had their wedding, and their anniversary was a day away. Gradey had a romantic dinner planned at the club for their special day. They strolled the long and winding shoreline while the sun was at its highest point. Kascey had on a straw hat to protect her from the sun's glare. Gradey wore his shades as the sun glistened through his sandy ash hair. He was shoeless and held her arm in his. The seagulls swarmed through the air and made croaking calls as they looked for food from above.

"I suppose that the water is freezing," she observed, yearning for a dip.

"Yes, I suppose. We will get a chance to test it. We have three days here."

"I know, and then back to the hustle and bustle. Why don't we just stay?"

"I do not know. Maybe try to keep your mind off it. We can later, I suppose. Look at the time. We had better turn around to see Mabel and Ethan."

"That's right," she replied hastily. They turned around and headed back to the villa. Kascey changed into a strappy sundress, blazer, and sandals, and completed the look with her broad-brimmed hat. Gradey respectably wore his khakis and navy polo shirt to meet his in-laws. They casually strolled along the stone pavements to the pool side of the resort and entered the restaurant.

Kascey noticed Mabel's bronze straw hat and Hermes bag on the table overlooking the ocean. "I see them over here," she said as they walked straight into the table. "Mum, Dad, hello, how are you?" she cried.

"Fabulous, fabulous," answered Mabel as she held Kascey tightly. "Ethan look, Kascey," she said.

"Hello, Kascey," he said as he hugged his daughter and greeted his son-in-law. "It has been some time."

"I know. Wonderful to see you, Mr. Kann," replied Gradey with a handshake.

"Same here. So did you folks have a good flight?"

"Yes, it was perfect," Gradey stated.

"And even more perfect now that we're all here together," Kascey added as she took her seat and the others sat.

"Well, we have a lovely room," commented Mabel. "You should see it. I think that we shall stay longer."

"Really? I am glad to hear it, and I hope that you will be comfortable there. We need to fly back on Sunday," Kascey replied.

"You are here now, and that is all that counts." Mabel, who was practical and hardworking, veered Kascey back on track. She had raised Kascey to know the value of a dollar; Kascey had learned her work ethic from her parents. There was so much energy as the family talked and chatted the whole afternoon about the days ahead, the holiday weekend, their anniversary, the past holidays on the island, Kascey's designs, and the factory.

"You have no idea how grateful I am that you can help out. There are more orders every day, and I have the new shows in February to deal with when I get back. And Gradey has the new tech company," Kascey said.

"That is right. I feel as though I have taken on a new job. This venture is a bit more hands-on," Gradey stated,

"I see. Will you be spending more time out in the Silicon Valley?" Ethan asked.

"Not in the long term, and it is hard to fly there right now even though we have to ensure the operational side of the agreement is on track. However, I do not anticipate spending much time there at the moment," Gradey replied.

"Good, because it is a lot farther away than New York and Quebec," commented Ethan. He always looked after Kascey's welfare and wanted Gradey to be there for his daughter.

"We will be fine, Dad," she reassured him.

"I know, I know. Well, it has only been a year, and I know how it can be on a young couple. We do not want the stress of the businesses to get in between you two. You are such a great couple," he said supportively.

"Thank you, that was sweet. We really appreciate it," replied Kascey. "Now, I am famished; are you hungry, Gradey?" Kascey asked.

"Sure, I can have something," he replied.

"We think that we will have the snapper and corn fritters," Mabel said.

"Sounds delicious. I feel like the crab salad, and I just love the key lime pie," replied Kascey.

"Fabulous. Why don't we order then?" Mabel said as she searched for the waiter.

The plates arrived and were filled with the orders. They sipped their margaritas and enjoyed the end of the week. It was habitual for them to spend the last few days overlooking the ocean and reminiscing about good times. It would be New Year's Day in two days and their anniversary in one.

"New Year's Eve will always be special," noted Mabel. "We were here last year, and you were gorgeous as you walked down the aisle to the water's edge in that beautiful gown, and Gradey was so handsome. The reception lasted all night after you two left, and your father had the worst headache the next day. I think that it was one of the best days of our life besides our own big day."

"That is right. It was an enjoyable time. Your wedding will always be remembered."

"Thank you, Dad. We were so happy to share the day with so many special people—people that we have not seen in a while and hope to see again someday," she replied.

Gradey nodded in agreement. "It is hard to believe that it was just a year ago. What a momentous day it was. I must admit it feels so much like yesteryear with so much time from then until now."

The family sat and reminisced over more times for hours

before retiring to their rooms. It was the denouement of a year, the experience of which, was difficult to be remembered. They looked forward to the festive private plans for New Year's Eve. It would be outdoors, and Mabel and Ethan were to join for drinks and treats after their dinner on the outdoor patio of the private resort. There would be mini tables surrounding the pool overlooking the bay that were socially distanced for the guests.

~~~~~~~~~~~~~~~

The euphoria of the holiday made the days appear to be phased into one. The happiness which was experienced turned the tables for Gradey and Kascey. It was New Year's Eve, and they sipped from their champagne flutes under the stars while listening to a steel drum band playing calypso in the background.

His eyes were set on hers. "Happy New Year, and anniversary," he said as he clinked his glass with hers.

"Happy New Year and happy anniversary," Responded Kascey, who was wearing a slim form-fitting red silk evening gown with red crystals embellished diagonally across the bodice. "I have to say I feel miles away from everything and that we have left the entire world behind. I cannot believe that in forty-eight hours we will be back in New York."

"I know. We are so used to it. Why don't we just think about what we have right now?" he said as the waiter brought in the first course. "Thank you. This looks great."

"Yes, thank you," Kascey responded as they brought in the seared scallops. "You are right. Can you believe that it has been a year? Look at how it all seems to have stayed the same since that beautiful day."

"I know. It was a beautiful day, wasn't it?" he replied. They could hear the carousing of revellers further down the beach as well as the crackling of the fireworks.

Ethan and Mabel were in their suite, enjoying a quiet dinner of lobster and champagne in their living room overlooking the ocean. The sun had set, and the sky was a deep purple as they peered from their balcony and saw the revellers along the beach. Ethan was dressed in his tuxedo, and Mabel in an evening gown, while they listened to the festive music.

"Listen to the music, I love the familiar sound," said Mabel.

"Yes. It reminds me of days previous visits. We should head down soon," replied Ethan.

"Sure. Let's sit down in the lobby for a drink before we meet them."

"Just like old times. It is going to be a wonderful night," he replied.

The celebrations were dispersed in the open space, and the night's air was cool with a slight breeze. They were dressed in their formal attire, ready to meet the romantic couple on the ground-floor patio in an hour or so. It was already ten thirty at night; one and a half hours of the year remained, and the countdown had begun.

~~~~~~~~~~

"Look at the time. Your parents should be here soon," Gradey calculated, savouring the last few moments that they had alone.

"Yes. I just want to thank you for all of this and for your understanding. This is so wonderful, and I could not think of a better place to see them after the past year," she responded appreciatively.

"You are so welcome. I am glad to be a part of it all and to be back where it all began for us."

"Me too," she replied.

After their main course, they relished the time until they were about to receive dessert, when Ethan and Mabel were expected.

"Hello. Why, Kascey, you look wonderful; that dress really suits you," her mother complimented her.

"Thank you. You look great too. I love that dress on you," Kascey replied as she rose to give both parents a hug.

"Hello Mabel, Ethan. Everyone is fit for the occasion, I see," commented Gradey.

"Hello, and yes we are. Looks like you have the dessert ordered," replied Ethan.

"Yes, it is black forest chocolate torte with raspberry and crème fraiche," Kascey replied. "Also a fresh bottle of champagne to bring in the New Year. I have to say that we are happy to see the end of the old one."

"Now, everything is a blessing and in its time," responded Mabel. She was very faithful and a firm believer in being appreciative.

"I know. We have ordered wonderful dessert, and the band will start the prompt when the clock hits midnight. I think there will be a small firework display."

"Perfect. The atmosphere is all so dazzling," replied Mabel. "It tastes delicious," she commented as she tasted the torte. The resort had planned a very reserved celebration with guest numbers much lower than in previous years due to social distancing.

"I know. It is really rich and moist. I suppose that I can try this at home," replied Kascey.

Within half an hour, the new year rushed in as the old was dragged out with the memories and the sorrow of what had been. There had been a trade in places and a renewal which on any other occasion would have been missed but was tonight experienced in greater proportion as a result of the harsh year. They felt as though the new year rushed in like a fresh breeze full of hope and revival for some. Kascey and Gradey had accomplished their first milestone as a couple, and they were with their own mentors as a couple. Kascey took pride in her parents' relationship and tried to emulate it.

A few couples went to the floor to dance the night away under the wide, star-speckled sky and colourful, effervescent fireworks displays. Gradey heard his cue, took her hand, and walked her to the dancefloor and held her close as they moved to the sound of the bass and the drums. They tried to concentrate only on positivity.

"I love this song," she said.

"Me too," he managed to say over the loud music as they moved to the beat. Mabel and Ethan also took to the floor and were enthralled with each other, as if they were newlyweds. The memories of past vacations reignited an old spark on the key that had been subdued for years. The general mood for the New Year was still muted. There was no overpowering energy, as if the crowds were still in their designated quarters. The interaction and vibrancy had diminished and there was a connection tonight to one's partner not seen since the last century. The guests had commented that the bright side of the past year was the improvement of family values, of what was important, with a renewed faith and belief and inner happiness for the unassumed aspect of life.

Kascey and Gradey stayed up until the sun began to rise. They watched it rise from their villa through the wide-open window. They had ordered some fish soup and johnnycake for brunch and were to spend the rest of the day lounging around the villa and on the beach. It was still a flavour that Gradey was becoming accustomed after a few holidays there. The tide was high, almost to the front lawn of the villa, and it was early in the morning.

"Let's take a dip in the water while the tide is high," suggested Gradey, "Come on; you do not know when we will get the chance again."

"Okay. I need my swimsuit," she replied. There were few

swimmers; most of the guests were still sleeping after a long night.

They slipped into the water and walked out until they were submerged in the sea shoulder height.

"A bit frigid," commented Kascey.

"I know; there is not enough sunlight yet to warm it up," replied Gradey.

The water was calm, and they swam further out to keep warm until they could no longer tolerate the temperature. Kascey hastily ran out and back to the villa, shivering.

"Now I am really awake," she stated.

"Me too. It was nice, though. Good for the circulation," he joked.

It was the perfect recreation to help them fall asleep until the afternoon, when they awoke to a strong breeze that had overcome the island.

"What time is it?" Kascey asked.

"It is almost two o'clock," Gradey responded subconsciously.

"Already? Have you heard from my parents?" she asked.

"No. I have been asleep like you. I guess they are all right."

"I will call them. Actually, should we order something?"

"Yes, please. However, we must pack. I cannot believe that our flight is tomorrow."

"I know. Luckily, there is not that much." She was almost eager to get back to the hustle and bustle of the city. The pandemic was subsiding, and there was no rush, but there were developments from the vaccine and a new show in six weeks' time.

"Well, I can handle it. You did it on the way in. It is so strange how quickly that time has passed."

After ordering her lunch, Kascey called her parents, who had stayed up late the night before.

"How are you both? We would have called earlier, but we were still napping," she said.

"We are fine, dear. We have been up a few hours and will probably have a quick bite later by the water if you want to join us," Mabel offered.

"That would be great. I have also just ordered something, as we were famished; however, we can meet you later by the pool to say goodbye. The weekend has really flown."

"I know, dear, and such a pity. It has been a lovely trip. We will miss you all, but we can talk more when we see each other," Mabel replied.

"Yes. Looking forward to it. See you soon." Kascey disconnected.

She felt a tinge of sadness as she saw Gradey collect his items and place them in the overnight bags.

"You are doing that too soon," she remarked.

"I know. I am just trying to get this out of the way. The flight is at nine a.m., and I just wanted to get a few things done in time," he replied.

"I understand. I am famished, though. The dancing last night must have burned calories."

"Last night was fabulous. It almost reminded me of our wedding. It was superb."

"I know. Our first anniversary."

"Well, there will be many more. Maybe we should come here every year."

"That would be a good idea. However, we have the businesses. Who knows where we will be this time next year? I could be opening a store in Paris, or you could be starting a new venture somewhere else."

"You know what, then?"

"What?"

"We have time now to just sit here and enjoy everything. We can visit at any time, not only the holidays," he concluded.

"Perfect. Sitting here and now is just fine," she agreed. They savoured the quality time together. It had been a strange year, and it had provided them a solid foundation on which to build the rest of their marriage.

The ocean swim had reinvigorated them after a long night. Kascey and Gradey sauntered to the open restaurant where Mabel and Ethan were seated, having also recuperated from the evening before. It was like a repeat of two days before, as they were in the same seats. Kascey and Gradey waved to her parents, who had donned their face masks.

Ethan waved back. "How has your day been?" he asked as they approached.

"Hi … how are you? We have had a very relaxing day. What about you? What are you two having?" Kascey asked.

"Just great. We are ordering some seafood salads again, and some fries," answered Mabel. "What are you two having?"

"I am not sure. Are you hungry?" she asked as she looked at Gradey.

"I could have a little something; I am still full. We have an early flight in the morning."

"That is right. We are so sad to see you leave. However, we have decided to stay longer," Mabel stated.

"Really, Mum?" queried Kascey. She was concerned about her orders being prepared.

"Yes. We are having such a wonderful time. We have the staff working on the orders, Kascey," she replied as she sensed a bit of trepidation.

"Thanks. I really did not mean it that way," she replied.

"So what are you two having then?" asked Ethan, changing the subject.

"We are having … the fish tacos. Right?" she said as she looked at her husband.

"Sounds good," he replied in agreement.

"Great. Let's order," stated Damian.

The music from the band in the background brought nostalgia of previous holidays as they watched the sunset over the horizon. Gradey and Kascey wrapped their anoraks, as a cooler breeze had set in.

"Chilly weather today. It is becoming a cool January," Mabel said.

"Yes, a very cool day. It will be colder in New York—about thirty degrees," Kascey said.

"Oh no. I suppose that Canada is the same."

"Well, I am quite pleased that all the orders made it out

in time for the New Year and now there are newer ones for the Epiphany celebrations and then Valentine's Day. This is what I like about this job. There is a style for every season. I can change the look with the climate."

"Yes, you have that privilege to create around the seasons, dear," replied Mabel.

Kascey did not want to say goodbye; and she wanted to sit there and let the time fill the void she knew that she would feel once she left them. The year ahead was still an uncertain one. She was unsure as to when they would be together again. She prayed for the spring and a change in circumstances, and she prayed for a better year. The other patrons of the restaurant had trickled out as the night set. There were stars above, coupled with the fresh sea breeze. She hugged her parents again for the New Year as they bade farewell. It was a long goodbye, as there would be an uncertain year ahead.

The evening turned dark, and the mystical cool breeze drifted over the shore as it was soon time to take flight. They awoke early and were driven to the airport, where they climbed the short stairway to the door of the chartered jet. Kascey looked around her one last time to view one of her favourite places that stood the test of time and brought so much happiness in her life. As they stepped in, they automatically reverted to their present-day lives. Gradey started to examine his cell phone and Kascey hers. The business executives had been reformed to their natural selves to enter life as they knew it.

"What time do we land exactly?" he asked.

"I think at about twelve, so we should be home at around one p.m."

"That sounds wonderful. I hate to leave here, though," he replied, being considerate regarding her feelings.

"I know, dear. I know," she stated.

The small jet took off, and as they elevated to fifty thousand feet, Kascey peered through the window to see the small resort from the air. In a few moments, it was all behind them and the island became a small speck from the sky. She thought of Mabel and Ethan and what a fabulous time they'd had just being in their element and reminiscing on old times. She was overcome by a calm balance. They had made new memories as mature couples together. Gradey continued on his phone while Kascey sneaked in a nap while airborne. The time flew on the plane, and she awoke feeling fully rested.

The plane landed on a cleared yet frosty runway and slowly made its way to the private terminal. They gathered their belongings and disembarked. Their car was waiting, and after a "Happy New Year" greeting, they had a smooth and quick ride to downtown Manhattan. Raul was at the entrance, eagerly awaiting their arrival as they were swooped in and up to their apartment. The familiar smell of the corridors and carpeting comforted them with a home sweet home feeling.

"Home sweet home again," she said, remembering her last arrival in September, which seemed to have been eons ago.

"I know. Back home. It has become such a nest for us during this whole ordeal," he remarked.

"I know, but I could have stayed a little bit longer, bearing in mind that I have so much work to do." Kascey realized that it was time to shed the nostalgia and buckle down to work.

"Tell me about it. I have mountains piling up again."

"I have a show in six weeks. It will be socially distanced again though, even though the vaccination distribution here should be farther ahead."

"Right. Let's try not to stress ourselves. I hope it is perfect, and best of luck with that. I am sure that you will be fine."

"Thanks for your encouragement. Now, what do you want to have? I can always make something, or we can order again."

"Let's just order in and do not bother yourself. What about that gourmet pizza place across the road?"

"Fine, I will find something to order." Gradey always wanted a New York slice when he had left the city for a bit, although this had been a short trip.

"Great. I just need a slice of the New York pizza."

She fumbled on her phone to make the order while he took the bags to the bedroom to be unpacked. She looked at the terrace and the familiar view and was once again mesmerized. It never ceased to amaze her. It was a chilly January afternoon, and the sun was dim and would not rise any more than its position at 1.00 p.m. There was snow forecast for the rest of the week, and with that there was so much to which to look forward. There were more dresses to compose and a new line for the autumn to create. It would be a serious January, and the world was still her oyster from her suite in New York. She anticipated less travel, but Paris was an option. She and Gradey needed a getaway, and this time, she did not want to leave him.

They were still uncertain as to whether Paris would be open for tourists.

"Did you manage to make the order?" Gradey asked as he entered the living room.

"Yes, Gradey, I have. Just what you wanted. Allow me to get the plates together, because they should arrive soon."

"Thank you, dear," he replied again, very appreciatively.

"You are very welcome." She knew that it was the least that she could do, as the next week would be very hectic. She wished that she were still with her family in the keys. "I just want to say how meaningful it was to be with my folks and you this New Year's. It was perfect," she said as she returned to the settee.

"Thank you. It was really an honour to be with you all again and to celebrate our anniversary. I am happy that we got a chance to see them and that it made you so happy," he replied.

They savoured their lunch behind the french doors overlooking the terrace as New York was freezing. They had made new memories in their beautiful apartment and celebrated a perfect and cosy homecoming. The tree lights were lit, and they had the beginning of the new year in their splendid apartment.

14 | Bring in The New

The fresh new air of January brought such promise. After complying with the protocols, Kascey and Gradey finally took the car to work and were dropped off at their doors. Kascey ascended the elevator to her design studio. It was the second week of January, and the last of the holiday orders had been shipped. She was early and combed through her emails. There were countless order confirmations. She came across an email from Moda wishing her a happy New Year.

Kascey explained, "Sorry, I have been so busy at work and we had a superb time over the holidays. I finally got to see my parents. Gradey is doing well." She had been so delayed in keeping up with her personal correspondence. Her old friends had all reached out to her over the New Year holiday. The new year was filled with such promise of what could be in the months ahead. Vasquez had thanked her for the holiday card, and her former neighbour, Nathalie, was still off work. Lucy sent a wonderful card, and Norsa wrote a legal update. Her optimism dropped again when she thought of the horrible ordeal. She waited for the conference call.

"Happy New Year! I trust that the new year finds you well," Norsa opened.

"Thanks, and the same to you. Yes, very well. We had a quality weekend with my parents, and I am starting fresh," Kascey replied.

"That sounds wonderful. Now, we have issued the injunction and the trading has stopped. So that was a victory. There has also been an action of breach of cyber security and data as well as damages in the amount of $12 million. That is the next step in the case. I know that you do not want to get too involved, and it will occur in a foreign jurisdiction where the actual incident has occurred. We have excellent co-counsel there working in that area of the world." Norsa updated her on the legal efforts made and provided a new strategy for the year. "We will have a conference with them later this week on prospects."

"Thank you, and I really appreciate it all. I have been eagerly awaiting the outcome of this ordeal, and the sooner that it is behind us, the better," responded Kascey.

"That is right. We are just going through the discovery of documents now, and we are liaising with your computer expert, Val, on this as well. We should have everything together in two weeks for a trial early in March."

"Right, then. and thank you. I shall prepare for that."

"That is great. And as always, we are here for you. If there is anything that you need or anything that may be of concern, just let us know."

Kascey hung up optimistic that this whole ordeal would

soon be over. She responded to her other emails and counted the inventory with Judee and Syre.

"Perfect, we have sent out most of the orders. We did not get one or two, but we will have to compensate them for that. How about a double order for the disappointment?"

"I am right on it," replied Syre.

"Perfect. The clients need satisfaction. It is key to this business. We need their loyalty," she determined.

"That is right. Customer satisfaction is key, and we have a few notes from the holiday season," added Judee. She read out the customer satisfaction replies and surveys, reporting on how they had enjoyed wearing the designs over the holidays.

"That is all so encouraging," Kascey said. "We must now think about the fall show in a few weeks. I have the designs ready; we just need to get to the manufacturers. Nothing is computerized yet, and they are hand-sketched. I have learned from the last mistake," she informed them cautiously. She pulled out her sketches and laid them out for the staff to review.

"Those look impressive, and I really like the motif," Judee confidently asserted.

"Thank you. It is going to be a slight grunge of a winter as people are coming out of this climate; however, it will be more glamorous as they head into the next holiday season and leave behind the semblance of what life was like once this is over. The frame of mind is to move on from the ordeal of the last year. So after a summer of our sheer designs, we will move into sustainable light wool cardigans, throws, tweed, and smooth, tall fall boots," Kascey explained.

"It really looks sophisticated, and I love those berets," Judee commented.

"Glad that you do. I also love these sweater dresses with the thigh-high boots. Look, we have them in every colour: deep grey, teal, burgundy, and mustard brown. I am trying to pull the colours from the tweed coats and fabrics."

"Oh it is so fall and comfortable," Judee replied.

Kascey continued on to explain every detail of the sketch and every swathe of fabric. She even suggested what would be best for each hair colour to accentuate the look. She arduously deliberated over the designs and the fabrics until it was time to bring them to life. She retrieved her shears and the fabric and started to cut. She placed the material together and sewed in a long stream for the throw. The fabric rested on her knee, and she felt the warmth of it and knew that it would keep her clients warm through autumn and next winter. Her day was spent in front of the machine until she had produced two or three items. She anticipated a late night and a hectic week to get it all done by the end of February.

"Look, I will close up here. I just want to get this all finished," she said as the staff started to wrap up for the evening.

"Well, let us know if you need us. We can always wait with you," offered Judee.

"No, that is fine. I am almost done here. We can work late tomorrow; this will go on all week."

"Okay, and have a nice evening. Call us for anything," said Syre.

Kascey worked for another hour while waiting for Gradey to arrive home before she left. He'd had a long day as well, and they would both be exhausted.

"I've some teriyaki here for dinner," she said as she walked through the door.

"Great! Thanks. How was your day?" he asked.

"It went well, actually. Not too badly. And you?"

"It was regular. I have to travel in the early spring to California again to check the site. Do you want to come this time?"

"No, I really can't, as much as I would like to. I have the shows again."

"Too bad." He was disappointed. "I would really like you to see the building."

"I thought that they would be moving from there," she answered. "Besides, how do you know it will be clear to travel then?"

"I know. They were but managed to salvage that portion in the negotiations, and there is no real designation to travel."

"I see. Next time, dear. Now, do you want some salmon teriyaki?"

They had a late meal until it was time to settle in for the evening. Exhausted, they clambered into bed and covered themselves with the warm duvet to protect them from the frigid January chill outside.

The rest of the week was one of optimism as they set their

resolutions of achieving goals and setting in place the strategy for the new year. Kascey still had her show and the case to complete. Gradey had a new IPO on the horizon and tough work to increase the market share of Tirogam. Although he would have preferred to stay in one place and virtually meet, there was more travel in the works to complete this heavy task. He also secretly hoped that he and Kascey would be able to have a secret rendezvous somewhere in Europe when their work obligations were alleviated. He felt the chill outside as the frigid wind blew and the temperature dropped overnight.

In late February, Gradey checked the financial statements and the statistics on the flight to California. It all appeared to be in good form. He had his agenda set to meet with Dan and Roger, as well as some of the staff. He was inspired by being in a new business and wanted to excel in every aspect of the tech industry. It was the world of tech that the financial analysts on Wall Street had once raved about. He yearned for the proverbial goose that laid the golden egg and would try to make this work. They would be coming out of it on top, and he could feel his pressure surge and his luck increase.

It was a short drive to the workplace location. "I am still impressed every time we come to the headquarters," he commented to Claude.

"I know. It is massive. Perhaps it is a promising idea to keep it now that the economy is opening; we have appreciation in value to anticipate."

"Yes, we had better have it noted in the books."

They were escorted to the executive floor to meet Dan and Roger. The building contained no more staff than it had in November as employees waved to them as they walked by. It was a more congenial response than last time, and Gradey felt more included in the team. The insistence of generating an amicable environment was part of the culture. The culture was more relaxed than the corporate enterprises he had dealt with before, but no less productive.

Dan and Roger were eagerly awaiting the arrival of their new company executives. The meeting was encouraging for an unpredictable start to the new year.

"I am impressed by the improvements," Gradey stated. "Ads have increased over the holidays, as have deliveries and purchases. I do think that we have turned the curve and that there is an optimistic outlook. Also, the expenditures have declined, and the value of the company is increasing."

"Yes, there have been many improvements," Roger explained. "We have part-time staff, which helped with the expenses, and contractual delivery couriers to meet the demands for the new market niche. Also, we have diversified the portfolio and have had a successful holiday season catering to those who were unable to get out this year."

"Yes, we can see the figures beginning to pick up," Gradey replied. "There is more work to be done as there was the January slump upon us; however, it is promising in the least."

"Well," interjected Dan, "we have been busy implementing

the proposals since last November, and it is rewarding to see the fruits of our labour."

"We can see that, and it is very appreciated. We took on this project because we anticipated an increase in the market share, and it is going that way until an anticipated return on investment in the spring," said Claude.

"Thank you; we appreciate it. Now, we have your offices all set up for the next few days so that you can audit and review the company procedures."

"Thank you and we appreciate it," Gradey said as they were escorted to a swanky suite with a view over the plush and plentiful lawn. "This is a great room, and this is a very calming view." He noted the difference between his Manhattan office and the serene feeling and vast pioneering promise of the West Coast.

"We thought that we would save the best for you. Anything that you need," offered Roger, knowing that this would be the last bout of hosting, as they were a very integral part of the company. Gradey had invested a significant amount to leverage in the company, and he was now a major shareholder and director.

"Well, thanks," added Claude as he set his case down on the large table in the suite in the wing of the building.

Gradey and Claude prepared for more virtual meetings with supervisors to ensure that the new objectives were being met and to address any issues that needed to be ironed. They were impressed with their reception and now felt an included part of the community.

"If anyone would have asked if I would have been in the Silicon Valley a year ago, I would have had to say that it was impossible," Gradey noted. "Now here we are in this massive building and sparse landscape in a completely new environment as executives."

"Unbelievable," Claude observed. "The world's events have changed this around completely. Luckily we were there for the taking,"

"Luckily," Gradey agreed, knowing that he was fortunate to have his family.

"A bit more than luck," Claude said. "You must have the keen eye and the talent and the sustainability to keep up with it all. Anyone can get you want you want, but you have to have the ability and the knowledge to make it a success. Nothing happens overnight just because there is financial backing. It boils down to you to make it a success, and with this project there is still hope."

"Yes, I guess that you are right," Gradey said with a little humility. Demanding work was a part of his fabric and he had an exceptional work ethic.

~~~~~~

Kascey arduously worked on her autumn line. Her show was in a few weeks, and they would once again travel to Paris for the show. She was still addressing the pandemic protocols even though many people involved were expected to be vaccinated. The shows in London would be online, as with Milan and

New York; however, the trip to Paris was necessary, as she wanted Gradey to join her.

Travel was opening up again and there had been too much time apart with Gradey's new project. There was lost time for Kascey and Gradey to regain. Kascey had planned a lively summer weekend in the cape with family and friends but it was too early to make any more plans. Gradey had not seen his close friends from college, Caleb and Ray, in a long time, and a summer break would cheer him up. Kacey had thought about inviting Lucy and her friend Trudy, but Lucy was expecting her baby to be born in a few weeks. She had not seen Moda in a while, and she and her husband, Remy, would be perfect to invite.

She picked up her phone, "Hi, Moda, how have you been?" she asked, uplifted.

"Great, thanks. I was getting worried, as we have not heard from you," she replied ecstatically.

"Not to worry. We are on track for the shows, and I am checking your availability."

"I have it all noted in my schedule, so whenever you are ready for the fittings."

"Great. We should be ready by next Friday. There is still a week to go. Also, what are you doing Labor Day weekend? I know that it is a bit far off; however, we are thinking about going to the cape," asked Kascey.

"That would be perfect. Thank you. I will note it down now so we do not forget. We are still a bit timid from the science of this whole thing, but I think that it would be better to travel by then," she replied.

"Great, and you can always drive. Now, have I told you? The case is heating up and should be over by April."

"That is great news. Anyway, that would be fabulous, and I know how much of a strain that this has been for you. We will have a celebration once the show is done," promised Moda.

"Yes, we will have to celebrate once we can see past all of this. We have survived thus far, and there is more of life to live."

"I know, and fingers crossed that it will all go as planned."

"Fingers crossed so we will see you in Paris anyway. You will love this motif. Think country life and a relaxed brisk fall atmosphere."

"That sounds impressive, and I cannot wait." They hung up knowing that there was a need to work again and to be on stage to present how she visualized the sentiments of her audience in the next few months. Not only was Kascey talented, but her work exemplified the moods of her clients and how to inspire them.

15 | Weekend Rendezvous

Kascey was completely frantic with two days to go until the Paris show. Gradey was flying with her, as promised and they had a flight to Paris. They were confident in travel after meeting the vaccine requirements and being tested again. Knowing that there would be major work amid the hustle and bustle to get there, she drew strength from past times, and with the city opening after a long winter, her excitement for the old Paris grew. It was odd how quickly the six months had changed the world. That being said, there would still be social distancing, and she planned again for a delightful open-air show. She had resorted to online shows in the neighbouring countries, but this trip was required, as it was once her home and she was researching branch locations.

"Have we all the designs packed and ready?" she asked her team.

"All ready. Even the velvet wrap gown which is the finale dress," replied Judee. It was red, a colour that suited Moda well. The show included other plums and rusts for autumn. It was the end of February and winter in Paris, and these colours would provide warmth in the current climate.

Kascey delved into shoes for autumn. She had produced boots and strappy sandals in the same fabrics as her gowns.

"Thanks a million. Don't forget the shoes," she replied. She had all sizes and shades just in case.

"No, we won't," Judee said. She and the interns, Marisol and Niquita, were hard at work to finish it all. They were interested in the industry and were Kascey's mentees, still studying fashion locally.

"We have to guard everything with our lives. I cannot rely on the couriers for those important pieces," she acknowledged.

They diligently itemized everything as Kascey went over the agenda and the roles of each model. She paired each model with each dress concisely and sent her the schedule. They worked until late in the evening. Kascey had already packed for the flight the next day and would burn the midnight oil until it was all completed.

"Now I think that this is everything," she said as she closed her computer at almost 9.00 p.m. "I will finish anything else from home. The flight is not until tomorrow morning."

"Right, and good luck at the show. We will be cheering from here," Judee replied.

"Thank you. I will contact you when I am onboard to confirm everything. Now, can you please help me to the car with the gowns?"

They packed the bags in, and Kascey guarded them as she was driven to her apartment. When she entered bogged down with parcels, she could smell the takeaway Gradey had ordered.

Raul followed with the others and helped her to place the bags in the foyer as she called for Gradey.

"I am in the study just getting some last-minute correspondence in," he answered.

"Okay. I am just sorting out the luggage," she replied. "There are more bags per person this time."

"Hi, dear. I see, and it looks like we will be a little overweight," he joked as he greeted her in the hallway.

"Looks so. I could not take the risk this time," she explained.

"I know. No need to explain," he responded understandingly.

"We will just have to pay overweight," she concluded.

"Right then. There is some dinner in the kitchen if you wish," he replied.

"That would be perfect. I am famished."

Kascey was accustomed to having a quiet evening before the flight to gather her thoughts. She tossed and turned as she thought about every scenario. By 6.00 a.m., she was up and ready for the nine o'clock flight. She gently nudged Gradey to awaken him, as they had automated themselves to get ready to make it to the airport in time. When they stepped into the car, Kascey was relieved and relaxed along the ride until she saw the terminals appear. Luckily at that time of the morning it was quiet and not crowded as they swept through check-in and security. Before they knew it, they were on the plane and seated. She had a long flight to check her agenda, as they were en route to the city of lights.

Their familiar hotel on the Rue Honore awaited, and they anticipated three days of devotedness. As they passed the monuments, Kascey was excited to see the familiar locations, from the Louvre to the Champs-Élysées, where she and Gradey would slip into side cafes and sit for hours or take an afternoon to visit the museums. The show was not that far from where they were staying and was booked in the sprawling courtyard of a large museum just on the right bank. Kascey felt as if she were back in her hometown after many years and once again with the man of her dreams.

She knew that she had really arrived as she viewed the Eiffel Tower. "Look; it is gorgeous tonight," she said as the taxi circled the plaza close to the hotel.

"That's right. It is all lit tonight," he answered. "The city of lights."

"Yes, we are in the city of lights together finally," she replied. "It is always so mesmerizing when you first arrive. The anticipation of the new journey begins."

"Is there anything that you want to do? I have booked dinner for two tomorrow night at your favourite restaurant just around the corner," he replied.

"Well, besides the show, just to spend time with you. And that was so thoughtful of you dear."

"I know. Besides the obvious, I just wanted to spend some quality time. I have taken these three days off, and I want this time to be perfect."

"It already is. I know that there is so much to do, but we will find the time," Kascey replied.

The car drove up to the entrance, and the porter arrived to open the door and collect the bags. "Bienvenus," he said as he opened the doors for them.

They disembarked and entered the lobby to check in. The new system was streamlined and quick as they hurried to their suite to settle their bags.

"It was all so easy this time," Kascey noted. "Look at this fabulous view," she remarked as she looked at the plaza.

"You are right; we can almost see the entire city, and there is the Champs-Élysées." He marvelled at the view. "Let's order something and just enjoy this."

"Okay. After that I have to get back to work."

"Yes, that is fine. We must enjoy it, though. Who knows when we will get back? These cities are closing so often now it might not be until the fall or even next year," he commented.

"Why don't you order something please? I need to check the inventory again," she replied.

Kascey itemized each piece and checked in with the models who had all met the entry protocols and would collect their separates in the morning before the show. She felt relieved that they were all there already and that by tomorrow evening it would be over. There was the NYC show in a few days, and that would be socially distanced again.

She and Gradey had dinner on the terrace. The trolley had been left outside the door, and Gradey rolled it into the room. They placed the settings on the patio. It was still rather cool, but they wanted to enjoy the scenery as if they were having a spring day. It was expected that the weather would be milder over the next few days.

"Bon Appetit," Kascey said delightfully.

"Yes, Bon Appetit," he replied as they savoured every morsel of their dish.

"I just feel so lucky that after all that we have been through, we can finally be here together and reminisce."

"I know. Truly, we should count our blessings. It was worth the wait. Almost a year ago, it was a tough prospect, and now here we are," he replied.

"Yes, here we are again," she replied. "This has been a second home at times, and I feel it is more than just a trip."

"I know. You have some history here," Gradey agreed.

"Yes, it is where I trained and learned to love fashion and life, and to celebrate the achievements," she replied.

They settled on the terrace for as long as possible before retiring to the settee for the dessert. It was already ten thirty in the evening, or four thirty on the East Coast. She would remain on Eastern time to arrange her show the next day and have a late morning. It was scheduled at three in the afternoon and still in Paris.

She looked at him. "You know what? I do not think that I could do this without you."

"That is reassuring," he replied as he put his arm around her shoulders. "Thank you."

Grady had not checked his emails that evening and had put the phone away until the next day. He would stay in the hotel and work while she was at the show.

"Promise me that you will watch some of it online tomorrow," she asked.

"Of course I promise; I would not miss that," he replied, knowing that she knew what he was thinking.

<hr>

The sun had risen early for a late winter's day, and the new day suddenly upon them. Kascey did not have as long a nap as she thought to recharge. She was eager to see the models as they collected the designs for the show. She would meet them later as they prepared with the stylists. It would be a repeat of the last time, and experience had been her teacher.

Moda, Chantelle, and Talia had arrived and were reviewing their items while feeling a rush of excitement for the show and, of course, to be back. Kascey was on a tight budget, and there was less travel for this season to cut costs. Many were still reeling from the recession. Her brand would produce the basics for work and country settings, as well as for those long walks on autumn nights from work in the city, and for time spent relaxing outdoors in the countryside. The autumn season was also good for shipping items appropriate for warmer weather over the holiday season.

She reviewed the items and the line-up and promised them that she would be arriving in a few hours to oversee the show. There was a tight agenda and a stellar line-up with hair and makeup to be completed. The runway scene would have more plums and roses, with futuristic slicked-back chignon hairstyle. A look of extremely high cheekbones complimented the motif.

"Now good luck, and take care. I will see you all later," Kascey replied. "Make sure to also give these to the other models," she instructed.

"Right, we will. Have a fantastic morning, and please say hello to Gradey," answered Moda,

"Yes, I will. See you soon, and thanks," replied Chantelle. They all dashed down the hallway and back to the lobby, where the car was waiting to take them to the show.

Gradey was half awake. "Morning. I see that you got sorted."

"Yes, I was with the ladies, getting the outfits sorted. Do you want some breakfast?"

"I suppose. Not right now, though," he said. He was a bit out of sorts as he finally picked up his phone. "What time is it?"

"It is almost ten in the morning, and I have to get prepared for the show by noon.

"All right, and good luck. Remember tonight. I want it to be special," he reminded her.

"Sure, and I can't wait, but it seems as though I have another world to get through before then."

"Take all the time you need," he replied as he calmly scrolled through his missed emails. Some were just arriving from the West Coast, as it had just turned midnight there. The project was on track and the share prices were increasing. The economy was a force to be reckoned with this winter, but as an essential provider, the business was faring well. The news of the vaccine had heightened the share prices of other main industries, such as hospitality and transport, and he hoped that the increase would also lift the price of Tirogam.

"Good news," he continued. "The share prices are up. I am on track to get my return on the investment."

"That is fantastic." Kascey was relieved, as she was beginning to miss him on his business trips.

"Thanks. We did it. I knew that we could," he said as he started to write to Claude. He was delighted that the share prices had increased because of the vaccine, and crude oil and solar energy shares were rising.

"Now, while you are concentrating on that, I am going to get ready for the show."

Kascey wore one of her designs—a wool wrap cocktail dress in stone grey with burgundy gloves and boots, and a grey fedora. "How do I look?" she asked as she exited the dressing room.

"Sensational. Just sensational," Gradey replied.

"Thank you. And now I must go. Don't forget to order something. Perhaps take a walk around."

"I am all right. There are a few things that I have to sort out. When will you be back?"

"I think that I will be back about seven or eight at the latest."

"Good, because dinner is at eight at our favourite spot just across the road from here," he reminded her.

"Perfect. I should be back before then," she promised.

It was hard to believe how quickly the trip was going; this would be their last evening. It was a real whirlwind romantic getaway.

"See you soon, and good luck," he replied.

"Thank you, dear." She whisked out the door and to her car waiting at the entrance.

~~~~~~~~~~

The mood at the venue was energetic as stylists and designers alike scurried around to prepare for this heightened event. Kascey surged with anticipation as she saw her models readying for the show. The line-up was a glamorous side of the 1930s—a reflection of the way that people overcame their issues and the strength that was exhibited through their style.

"I love it. It all looks fabulous," she encouraged the entourage as she entered.

"Thank you," replied Moda as the other models smiled and nodded.

"Here we go again," Kascey said, starting a pep talk. "You can perform as we have done before. Everything looks perfect." She clapped with enthusiasm as she walked past. "Remember your line-up."

Her collection was being exhibited on a mild March day and outdoors. The new normal was not as challenging after her experience in the autumn. It seemed a repeat as the models again marched and portrayed the designs on the catwalk. When the final call was made, she joined them. Again, her slight frame appeared in contrast to their very tall figures. The show was a success, and she was invigorated by the applause from the industry. She was on cloud nine and inspired by the atmosphere, the modern style of the collection, the perfect Parisian day, and the energetic vibe of the industry. She felt as if it was where she wanted to be and that her demanding work had paid off. The show was also aired online so that her colleagues and clients could watch from the comfort of their homes. It was no longer fully exclusive, and sales would rocket. The team back in New York were eagerly awaiting the surge in orders.

She called Gradey. "Did you watch it? Did you like it?"

"Yes, it was fantastic. I loved it. Now remember to meet me at eight."

"I will do dear; I will do." The concept seemed easy enough, as it was only five thirty. She called her staff in New York to get their assessment of how it had looked.

"Well, we loved it and have been cheering you all on," Judee informed her. "The colours blended very well on the stage, and the innovative aspect was amazing. We have orders already for some of the evening dresses for the late summer balls. We loved the way that the holiday evening collection was presented. We have orders coming in for them as well."

"Fabulous. Thanks for the reassurance, and we have more work to do back at the studio. It is getting late here, so we are all going to pack up and get the dresses back to the hotel."

"See you when you return, and good luck with the flight," replied Judee.

"Thank you, and see you all in a few days." Kascey was

adamant, as she knew that the orders were coming in again after the show. Her expectations were again inspired by the success of her line. She realised how blessed she was to have survived the past year and not to have failed before she started. The ladies packed the collection and moved the bags to the suite before saying farewell. They had planned a small gathering, which Kascey would have to leave early as she was meeting her faithful and endearing husband.

Gradey sat at their regular table close to the window near rue Saint-Honoré. He took in the atmosphere and pondered the last time that they had been there. It had been a year and a half ago. It was summer, and Gradey and Kascey had a secret rendezvous weekend to Paris before their wedding. She had sat in front of him as his bride to be, and he had felt like the most honoured man in the world. He sipped his aperitif and perused the menu. He checked his watch. She had five more minutes to appear.

She appeared in a black cocktail dress at the door with her satin burgundy gloves and handbag and tall black boots. Her hair had been swept to the side, and she wore her designer mask as she walked to the table.

He knew that it was her in an instant as he rose to greet her, "Hello, darling, thought that you would be late," he said, impressed.

"Not for you, dear. I am right on time. Anything for you," she responded appeasingly.

"You look absolutely dazzling tonight; I love that," he replied.

"Thank you, and so do you," she said as she took her seat. What are you drinking?"

"Just a little solace drink after being alone this afternoon," he replied, warranting pity.

"Sorry about that. I am here now."

"Not to worry. I had a lot to do. Besides, the show went great and you looked good out there," he reassured her.

"Did I really?" she asked, relishing the compliments.

"Yes. I would say. Congratulations! Now, can I order something for you? What will you have?"

The couple dined in the familiar atmosphere amid the classic Parisian decorations. There were cloths on the table and portraits on the walls, along with the playing of the familiar music. Paris seemed open again for the time being, and they were relishing their experience. They sat and dined until late, not wanting to leave. Their flight was later in the day, and they would make up time as they jetted across the Atlantic and into their own time zone.

After dinner, they strolled back to the hotel and took in the scenery from the penthouse suite one last time.

"When do you think we will be back?" she asked.

"I am sure that you will be back. As for me, it will be some time. There is not enough in the budget to have a business trip here soon," he replied, not wanting to dwell on the topic too much after what happened with his last venture there and the financial fiasco two years prior.

"I understand. Let's just enjoy this moment then," she conceded.

They wrapped up on the chaise longue and fell asleep under the Parisian lights. The city was magical, and their last evening memorable. It stood out like the others, and they made new memories in their old city, not knowing when they would return.

16 | New York Minute

New York had opened even more when the pair returned, and the prospect of optimism had reentered the city with the vibrancy of the city returning. Kascey and Gradey enjoyed the clear, springlike day as they drove to their apartment from the airport and once again ascended the lift to their co-op on the twenty-fifth floor. The Lower Manhattan view was welcoming and vast as the mild sun illuminated the afternoon. Everything was still in its place after their few days away, and they took comfort in that continuity.

Kascey habitually settled to do the unpacking and the rearranging, while Gradey once again disappeared into the study, eager to see what he had missed over the past few hours. Since it was lunchtime in New York, and morning on the West Coast, he had a long day to which to look forward.

"I'll be in the study for a bit," Gradey said as he walked through the apartment's living room.

"Right then, I am just going to sort a few things out. I won't be going in tomorrow, and I still need some rest from that whirlwind trip." It had been swift and hectic, but she had achieved her goal. The show had been watched by over fifty million viewers around the world, and there were orders to fill. Finally she felt like a household name.

"You do that, and I will see you in a little while," Gradey replied, not wanting to wedge a gap between them after such companionship and romanticism.

"Okay, hon," Kascey replied in reassurance.

Kascey sat and productively flicked and scrolled through her phone that afternoon, ensuring that every email was read and dealt with accordingly. She was meticulous in her responses and decisively catered to each customer request. Business had become such an integral part of her life, and she did not know where she would be without her motivation. She felt a determination to correspond back and forth with the studio all afternoon, as if she might have driven to work.

Kascey connected to Norsa Shone from her own remote station, who exemplified a figure of hope who exuded confidence. Kascey again enjoyed the conference call as she listened to the update of her case. She was in a win-win situation by March, and the trial was in a few weeks. March had always been a cherished month for her, and she wanted the trial all wound up by the spring. It was filled with sunnier days and a fresh exuberance, with lighter clothing and inspiration, and Kascey hoped that life would soon be back to normal. She took that optimism to the meeting.

"We will have a video link to the hearing," Norsa informed Kascey.

"Really? It is incredibly surreal to be able to sit in on something halfway around the world."

"Yes. It is one of the positive aspects of the pandemic. Val will give his evidence, and your statement has been submitted. After hearing from the respondents, we will get the decision on the damages. It is a matter of protocol. There is a prosecution hearing in a few weeks from their authority regarding the criminal aspect. However, our role is extremely low in that regard. We want the victory over the loss of sales to your brand so that you can obtain your damages."

"Great, and I am looking forward to getting this over and done."

"Now, let me know if there are any concerns. I think that we have an exceptionally good chance of winning if it all goes as planned."

"That sounds really promising. I sincerely hope so," Kascey replied with a hint of trepidation. She and her team were really the pursuers in the case, and it was a little fearful at times. "What if we lose?"

"We will have to appeal. Now, I have set out the probabilities of that happening, in my opinion, and the next steps to consider in the event of a loss. We will not concentrate on that road until we actually do lose. I need you to stay positive."

"I will try," Kascey promised, managing to conjure up a brief smile.

Once the call had concluded, it was one aspect of Kascey's day out of the way. She only had to wait until March 20 and it would all be over. It was only the first week in March, and it seemed as though her life was settled on the spring and summer and Labor Day weekend. State mandates on social distancing had been relaxed. She grew more optimistic as spring arrived, with a soaring attitude and aspiration. She had hope that it would be a good year after all.

Kascey had a new aspiration and envisioned a cosmetics line that she was establishing which had taken up more time than expected. She had hoped to launch it by the holidays, along with her holiday collection. She was using the budget from the show in September to go towards the production and had meetings to analyse the research and development.

Gradey had settled in quickly after a few days out of the office, and it was a very promising day. He had spent it in the study and had witnessed a further increase in the share price for Tirogam. He also noticed an improvement in the new biotech company that they were investing in, which was situated in Massachusetts. The new company had been at the forefront in the fight to curtail the pandemic and, it had been assessed as a good opportunity. The share price was rising, and it was for a very pertinent cause. He felt his confidence surge as he read the financials about the new investment. The pandemic had shifted those who had become galvanizers in the fight to everyday people. He was one of them seeking to assist. His vison and purpose had changed dramatically and even stretched the limits of his personality to greater levels of consciousness and altruism.

Such attributes were attractive to Kascey. She could see the impact of the current climate on Gradey and was certain that, owing to his personality, he was the right person for her. She never looked back from the time that she met him, and she was confident in her marriage.

The days wore on throughout March until the new hint of sunshine and the promise of spring entered the living room. It was a new season—a lighter one full of promise. There was a shift towards a more structured lifestyle which was not like their previous lifestyle, as there were still the remnants of the casualness and the easy computerized access to people. The occasional drift back to the lounge environment was certainly being replaced by the hustle and bustle of a new life.

It was the thought of this new life that distracted her. Gradey wanted a child, and his sister Lucy would soon give birth; however, Kascey had so many dreams to achieve with the fashion house. Her dreams of a family were put on hold, as much as she wanted the scamper of tiny feet and someone wrapping himself or herself in her fabric, as she did at her parents' business. It would be delayed as she concentrated on her fashion house.

The day was bursting with spring and was business as usual. The staff worked diligently with fittings and filling the new orders inspired by the climate. The family's manufacturing company in Canada provided assistance, and it was overburdened after the show with filling the latest orders for the autumn collection.

"Have those orders been sent to Boston?" she asked as she scrolled through the list.

"They are next," assured Judee.

"Perfect. I see that the department store is asking for almost double the amount," she noted as she scrolled down.

"Yes. I think that they anticipate things getting back to normal up there soon."

"That is promising news. Things are finally turning around. This recession needs a boost."

"You are right about that," concluded Judee.

She decided to call Gradey, who was diligently glued to his seat and computer, following the markets. The stock price had risen again on the hopes of a new COVID therapy and vaccine.

"Well, it is not always good news for the tech companies, because people will revert to the traditional methods and industries, which see more of an increase," he explained to Kascey.

"I see. So when do you think that things will turn around fully?"

"It is difficult to tell. There has been at least a second wave, and there could be another one. We just have to be patient."

"I see," Kascey replied despondently.

"I know that it will take some time. Perhaps by the early summer now." He said this cautiously.

"I am only trying to figure out the best way to dress people—how to make them feel confident and gorgeous at the same time. I need to know the climate in which we are working."

"I understand your anticipation. Just carry on as you do, and things will be better," he encouraged her. He did not want to disenfranchise her so early in the year. "It is still relatively early in the year, and things will be better soon."

"Thanks, dear. Will you be finishing early today?"

"I should be at about six, why?"

"Nothing. Just wondering how to plan the day. It is all good news on the legal front, so I thought that I would make something special tonight."

"I am looking forward to it," he replied.

Kascey was satisfied that their life was improving. There had been times when they could just sit and reflect on the world's events and their lives for hours during the latest lockdown. She buffered the anticipation of further restrictions by solidifying her connections universally. Kascey intended to counter it by commissioning her manufacturers in her former countries to complete her orders. Gradey had developed main interests in other states and utilized those connections to get through.

"Why don't we just go to the Catskills or the cape for a weekend in a few weeks?" she asked.

"Sounds like a novel plan," Gradey said as he sipped his evening lager.

"I know. This day has been full of twists and turns, and we can get through whatever materialises."

"Yes, we can get through whatever the outcome. Like we did the last time."

Now that March was fully in operation, the evenings were lighter and the mornings were brighter as the bitter chill of winter receded into a warm spring glow. There was still cool weather, but not as much to worry about. Kascey's spring collection would still take effect. Her signature loungewear resurged. The orders had been placed during the previous autumn. However, the market was preparing for people going back to work, and her fashions had to evolve into that frame of mind.

"I wonder how I anticipated this? This collection was to be about liberation, not the curtailment of flow."

"I guess that is why you put the movement in the clothing—to counter all of that," Gradey suggested.

"Perhaps." She grinned at his sarcasm and his new knowledge in fashion.

***

Once the March madness had escalated and it was late in the month, the city was almost back to normal again. Everyone had come to terms and adjusted from the previous year, and the fresh flowers brought hope and renewal. Kascey was nervous about the case and concentrated on overcoming that hurdle. She had decided she would be watching via video link from the comfort of the studio. She dressed conservatively, with a white silk blouse under a tailored navy suit. She decided to wear her brunette bob away from her face; circle-rimmed glasses completed the professional look.

Norsa arranged a pre-appointment session to give Kascey a basic explanation of the process of the hearing. Kascey understood that although she was present, it was not necessary to testify, as her statement had been submitted and the expert evidence would come from Val. It seemed manageable enough, as she was a novice and might have made a mistake. She wore her external noise-muffling headset to be fully dedicated to what was occurring. The duration was a few hours and possibly another day—for which she was not required to be present, as her lawyers would be present for the ruling on damages.

"Now remember, just send me a message if you have any concerns, and I will address it. It is pretty much listed how it will all occur. Cheer up; we are hoping for a win," instructed Norsa.

"Thanks. I am a bit nervous, and it is difficult to believe that this can happen with modern technology."

"I know. Everything has changed. Good luck, and talk to you after the hearing."

The hearing started very formally, and Kascey was automatically transferred from her screen to the location. There were people in robes often speaking in a various language in boxes around the screen, along with interpreters. It was difficult to see the culprits. She was protected from being in the same room and on screen; however, the ringleader appeared very unassuming. She realised that finally she had come face-to-face with the person who had caused so much grief and hardship and that she should receive her compensation. She felt protected from a distance and was relieved for the remote hearing.

The respondents had to state their names for the record before the case was presented in opening statements by her lawyers. This was a civil case for damages, and the respondents then made their response. Norsa reiterated that she had to prove that it was reasonably foreseeable that the damages would result from the breach of cybersecurity data, and that the business had suffered a loss as a direct result of the breach. Her lawyers set out in chronological order the events that had occurred and the result of the loss. The evidence presented by the technical experts apparently connected the incident directly to the plaintiff. Further, exhibits were presented of the respondents' metadata and IP addresses, as well as the defunct website and registration used to sell the designs.

The designs sold on the website were identical to those that were created by Kascey and reproduced at a later date. There was so much evidence regarding dates and timings, and with the time zone difference, everything had to be considered and presented. The sales receipts relating to revenue, financial valuation spreadsheets, and the data on the loss of customers to Kascey's collection were also submitted in evidence. Kascey viewed patiently as the evidence was presented, hoping that it would be adequate.

The respondents argued that they had created their own designs and, although similar to the complainant's, they had no connection and had not used any of her data. They were resolute in their defence that it was merely coincidental, that their revenue had been obtained fairly, and that it was unforeseeable that the collection would cause a loss to the business of a plaintiff on the other side of the world. Kascey silently grew infuriated as she witnessed their audacity.

She watched intensely and realized that she had a precedent case in the making and that the outcome would ring volumes in the legal field. Many had tried to fight before and had lost because investigations into data breaches were very intricate. Also, the defence of remoteness of foreseeability and probability was so strong thousands of miles away. However, it was presented that these were seasoned offenders with seasoned tactics, and Kascey was not prepared to let anyone get away with the data theft related to her collection and brand. She sat, listened, and waited patiently as both sides presented their evidence.

She grew impressed with Val, who had done a superb job of presenting the evidence. It seemed strange to watch him from the sidelines, knowing that he was her technician. However, his expertise was stellar as he navigated through the witness statements and the questioning by the defence. Still, the respondents maintained that they had nothing to do with the data theft and the infringement of the style of the designs. It grew complicated as the verbose arguments were presented. She was out of her league in the legal verbosity; however, she persevered until the last argument was made.

By that time, it was almost 4.00 p.m., and Norsa and her team consulted with Kascey to explain any discrepancies.

"Thanks for all that you did today and for presenting my case," she said. "What happens next?" She listened intently and unreservedly.

"Now that the evidence has been presented," Norsa replied, "we will wait for the decision, which should come in no more than a few days, and we will keep you posted. Let me know if you have any more questions. This new form of hearing is unique and still evolving, and it felt peculiar. However, the respondents were overwhelmed, in my opinion. Even though there is a slight chance of loss, this should be an uncomplicated case because we had so much evidence in our favour," she replied confidently.

"Right then. All we can do is wait now," Kascey replied, resolved that the day had gone as planned.

"Yes, and we will get back to you. Please stay calm and try to get on with your life as usual. It is all in the hands of the court system now."

"Thank you, and I will keep in touch." Kascey turned her system off as she collected her thoughts, packed her iPad, and locked up the studio. It was late, and the staff had already left the building during the conference. After a seemingly nail-biting afternoon, the studio was empty. There was that empty feeling again that she may be walking out for quite some time, and she hoped that it was not to be the case.

It was still light as she walked to the apartment. It was a long walk; however, she needed to collect her thoughts. Now that she was almost certain of her reward, she deliberated on what she would do with the money. She thought that she could have another branch somewhere and that perhaps it could be on the West Coast, where she seemed to be losing her husband every month or so. Perhaps in Canada, or even Paris. The world had suddenly become her oyster after the turmoil that she had experienced. It was a reasonable sum, and she would have to invest it in some good.

She walked into the living room, and there was Gradey, as expected. He had dinner laid out. "Surprise, dear. How was your day?"

"Hello, this is for me? Thanks. Well with the case, it is what it is, but they are hopeful. You should have been there. It was so surreal, with the judges and lawyers and those culprits that make my skin crawl. Really, it was something else," she explained.

"Well, it is behind you, and you got through it. Now look, I have ordered your favourite from Pinelli's."

"Thanks, dear, this all looks wonderful. That is so sweet of you."

Gradey tried to create a relaxing environment after what he knew was a hectic day at work. They were very accustomed to their own companionship as they enjoyed their meal. They were looking forward to the summer holiday weekends in a few months, when they would see their friends again and take a break from the busy days.

The following day, Norsa called Kascey, overjoyed to inform her of the good news about the ruling. She was brimming with enthusiasm and excitement.

"I have some fantastic news. The judges have confirmed that there was a breach of data security and that there was a definite loss to your brand resulting from that breach," she stated.

"That is relieving news." Kascey replied.

"I must continue that they stated that you suffered a loss resulting from that breach and should be rewarded the said amount in damages of twelve million dollars and costs of the application."

"That is splendid news. We got it, and we did it!" she replied, overjoyed.

"Yes, we did it, and now we just have to submit the documents to court receive the award. Congratulations, and I know that it has been a long journey, but we have been successfully vindicated, and you have received the amount that you lost plus the pain and suffering."

"Perfect. That is brilliant news. Brilliant news. Thank you so much for all that you have done."

"You are very welcome. It has been a pleasure to represent you, and now there is the criminal trial for the defendants. We really do not have a key role in that, as they are repeaters in their own jurisdiction. It is the prosecution who are submitting the evidence. If you have any questions, then please let me know. This part is over, and you are entitled to your claim."

"Thank you. I have to tell Gradey and the staff the good news."

"You do that, and we will talk about the details at a later date."

"Perfect. Speak to you soon."

Kascey hung up vindicated and pleased with the outcome. It had been a long haul, and with the patience that she needed, it had been worth it. She spoke to her husband first and then to the staff. They were overjoyed and pleased that their arduous work had gone towards the fight. It was the first battle towards justice for her, and soon, with any luck, the culprits would be out of her life forever. It did not change the fact, though, that she still had to look over her shoulder. The effects of the episode had a psychological strain. She had developed little habits to ensure her safety and would check her computer with Val every other day. She was overly concerned with being careful with what she shared. The damage had been done, and now she needed her husband's advice on what to do with the award.

"Should I reinvest it or save it?" she asked.

"Well, if you want an appreciation on it, it is best to invest it, or to be more conservative and save it with a good rate," Gradey advised.

"Perfect then. I will look at the investment tools available. I really want to consider a new branch. What do you think?"

"That is a perfect idea. Perfect. A new branch where?"

"Either LA, Paris, or Toronto," Kascey informed him.

"Sounds good. You can have mobile offices as well. Not all have to be physical. I will leave it up to you," he replied.

"Thanks, dear. I have so much to think about now."

"Well, we have the time," he responded.

The restrictions were alleviating. Kascey and Gradey planned for the next few weeks until their weekend away.

17 | Spring Break

A warm spring had generated the blooming of an array of colourful flowers in the garden in the Catskills. Kascey and Gradey spent the weekend at their picturesque refuge, cleaning and gardening around their lodge. Kascey had the ambitious task of planting hydrangeas, azaleas, lilies, and roses, as well as cabbage, lettuce, and carrots. It had always been a dream of hers to have a beautiful garden, and she pruned her fresh flowers as she conscientiously dug and planted more seeds. She wore her overalls, a large straw hat, and her gardening gloves in the picturesque setting.

"Can you see that beautiful view?" she said, admiring the newly sprung flowers across the garden.

"It sure is magnificent," Gradey said, breathing in the fresh air as he sat on the veranda with his phone, overlooking the garden among the backdrop of the country woodland.

"Are you going to do that all afternoon?" Kascey probed him. "Why don't we take a vigorous walk to the village and get some exercise?"

"Sure, that is a great idea. Sorry, it is just that the share prices have finally increased and I can sell some to pay back Dad as promised."

"I see. That sounds very promising, but do you have to do it right this minute?"

"No, dear. Just a second as I get my hiking boots."

He disappeared into the quaint cottage for a few moments and then emerged with his boots and anorak.

"Here they are," he said as he pushed his feet into the boots and slipped his arms hastily into the sleeves of the anorak. "Right then, are you ready?"

"Yes, as ready as ever," she said as she slipped on her coat and took off her gloves. They walked through the back garden and through the trail filled with blooming buttercups and spring flowers to the main road. The view of the store grew closer as they dashed across the street to their favourite gourmet store. Kascey loved being able to specifically purchase items that were a novelty to take back to the city. Such items were now scarce; however, on her list of favourites were truffle sauce, freshly made juices, spring water, homemade spaghetti, freshly cut Stilton and swiss cheese, and organic baked goods. She looked around in wonder as she decided on her purchases.

"All of this is so tantalizing, but I do not see as much here. Do you want to select something from the buffet for dinner?"

"Sure. What would you like?" he asked.

"The salmon looks good with some fresh veggies," she replied.

"Right, I'll get it." He hovered over the buffet, selecting

it, as warm fumes from the sweet honey and garlic glazes rose from the dishes. "Do you want some of this salad?"

"Yes, please," she said excitedly as she shopped for more upstate homemade dressing.

"I think that I have everything now. Ready?"

They walked out of the quaint entrance with their purchases in recyclable grocery bags. The sun grew dim as it sunk to a lower 4.00 p.m. height. They relished the comforting feeling of being locals in the peaceful town as they acclimated to their new village. It was the intention to have a new location to resort to when they needed a break from their reformed city. As they walked to their long and winding driveway and started to climb the hill, Gradey's phone buzzed. He quickly checked it.

"That is amazing. It looks like the stork has arrived for Lucy," he said excitedly.

"What? Are you serious? That is fabulous news. I am so happy for her. Is it a boy or a girl?" she replied.

"Just wait while I get all of this ... Yes, it is a girl, Annabelle Rose, after our grandmothers."

"That is wonderful. What lovely names, and she must be over the moon."

"I know, and she weighs seven pounds and seven ounces and has hazel eyes and brown hair," Gradey informed.

"What a precious soul," Kascey replied, sounding touched.

"Now we have new roles. Just like that. We are to be godparents and uncle and aunt to this precious little baby." He turned his phone to display a picture. The baby was already in a pink crochet cap and embroidered cotton jumpsuit.

"Oh, she is so precious. Look at her. You can see that she looks a bit like you all—and then Nate, of course," she said, almost cooing.

"Yes. I would say that she looks so much like us. That's so perfect. We need to call Lucy and congratulate her when we get in."

The dim glow of the afternoon sun still provided warmth as they headed up the driveway on what remained a perfect spring day. It was full of hope and renewal, with a perfect blue sky. The flowers around the driveway had bloomed and scented the air. Kascey delicately unpacked the items and placed them on the kitchen counter and in the fridge to keep fresh until it was time to transport them to the apartment in the city.

"Please don't let me forget these," she instructed. "Now, are we going to call Luce and congratulate her?"

"Yes, let me get the phone." He collected the phone and video dialled her number. She was still in her scrubs and in hospital with Nate and their parents.

"Hey Luce, how are you feeling?" he asked, sounding excited and concerned at the same time.

"Great. Did you hear?" she asked.

"Yes, and we just want to congratulate you. We think she is gorgeous."

"Thanks. It all happened suddenly. Nate had to bring me in last night, and I called Mom and Dad."

"Well, congratulations," added Kascey. "This is brilliant news, and we are so happy for you," she replied.

"Thanks, that is so sweet. Do you like the name? Did you see the photo?" she asked, sounding concerned.

"Yes, it is all lovely. A great name, and she is beautiful; looks like the family," Kascey responded.

"Thanks," she said, looking smitten. Nate chimed in, and then Kelly, who was in the room and doting on her new grandchild.

"We are all here, Gradey," Kelly called out. Where are you?"

"Well, we are a bit far in the Catskills, or else we would see you. Since there are still restrictions on visitors in the hospitals, we will wait until you get out next weekend to see her," he explained.

"That would be fine," said Lucy. It was apparent how close she was with her brother; she wanted him to share in their joy and happiness and to introduce them to his niece.

"See you all then, and take care of yourself," he said as they disconnected.

He was overjoyed and proud. Kascey had not seen him this happy in a long time.

"The year is finally pulling together," she said.

"Yes. Let us celebrate. What shall we have?" Gradey said as they prepared for a cosy and quiet Saturday together in the countryside. They celebrated with wine and dinner from the gourmet deli and newly bought eclairs. The warmth of the sun had turned to a chilly March evening. It was late in March, and Easter would soon be there. They planned a quiet

Easter weekend together and decided to stay put until the early summer.

"I feel like it is March madness again," Gradey said.

"Finally," Kascey replied as they ensconced themselves on their settee and relaxed until the morning hours. When she awoke, the TV was still on and they walked to the bedroom to get some rest.

Back in the city, Kascey thought that she would get a general consensus regarding her next business move from her mother. She still valued her opinion, as she had many years of retail experience. Kascey had consulted advisors and wanted to ensure agreement.

"I think it is a perfect idea to expand," Mabel said.

"I know. I can have branches now. Can you believe it? I want one in Paris and one in LA."

"That is the way to go. Perfect cities. Why, even have one here, near our business address, and we can oversee things for you. It seems as if here is where we have been helping to assist your orders, and we have rapport with you already."

"That is what I will do with some of the money after donations. I will branch out." She cherished the notion of having her brand located around the world. There would be one branch in her hometown and one in her former hometown of Paris, as well as her husband's new venture area in California. She thought about the West Coast and the magnetic beach lifestyle and what she could create for women to wear in that environment. The style would vary from that of the Northeast in many ways because of the climate. She would have to consider the various shades to reflect the climate as well as the texture of the cloth and style. Paris would be a challenge— one that she had accomplished before. She remembered her days there and the intricacies needed to set up in fashion. It would require the expertise of an international corporate lawyer to do the paperwork, and luckily, she knew someone perfect—Norsa.

"I am going to realize this dream," she told Gradey that evening. "I mean, work is picking up for you, and we can travel to these places together. You can travel for your work and me for mine," she explained.

"I realize that," he replied. "However, this is more than being an investor. You will be an owner with a presence, and that takes regular overseeing. It is better to partner with offices in those locations first. A minor step to your dream." He was also genuinely concerned about her moving to different locations when they lived in New York.

"Perhaps that is the best way to start out, but wouldn't it be fabulous if I could just have my own dreams with my own branches?"

"Yes. As I said, you would need Norsa or a specialised person to advise you. It is possible. However, there is the issue of finding trustworthy staff who will have to carry these locations in your absence. Registered offices are a better idea. You have the presence with half the stress."

She listened to him and realised that this was one of the

reasons why he was where he was. He knew what he was talking about. She could still realize her dream. She would look for partnering offices and still run the operation out of NYC and stay rooted to her home and family life.

"All right, the success of the line will lead them to their own jurisdictions."

"That is right, and then you can determine which are lucrative before you plunge head-on," he continued his advice.

"Thank you for your wonderful advice; you are so knowledgeable. Now, what time will you make it home?" she asked, changing the subject.

"I think that I will be there by seven or so. Order what you like, and you can leave my dinner on the table please. By the way, I just spoke to Caleb, and he is so psyched about that weekend. He has a new lady in his life—Peronia."

"Good news. On Labor Day weekend, there will be six of us then? Including Jane, who has offered to do the cooking."

"Yes, and I hear that the surf is up," he replied. "I need to get back to work to sign off these shares to Dad. I am finally paying him back from his investment. See you soon."

"See you soon." She hung up and excitedly told the staff her plans for autumn.

"Does that mean that we will have to travel?" asked Judee.

"No, not at all for now. Mostly just me until they become profitable."

"Well, that is perfect news. We should get twice the orders now that we will have a perfect reach."

"Yes. That is the intention. I want to reach my customers

directly." Her mission was imperative, and she was dedicated to see it through.

They were on the cusp of the summer, which brought brighter evenings, as she locked up the studio where all her dreams were made. Her hopes and aspirations sprang one after the other in the building. Life was finally looking positive, as she could plan further ahead. There would be more stores in her business empire now, and as the old saying goes, "Out of bad some good comes."

18 | The End of Summer Wine

The hazy days of summer almost had passed, and Labor Day weekend approached quickly while the summer solstice had entered a new sphere as the season was on the brink of change to a cooler autumn. The concept of moving forward and renewal returned while Kascey and Gradey enjoyed the quality drive to the cape for the long weekend. They had opened the top of the convertible as they enjoyed the breeze and steered towards their destination. Kascey had stacked the back seat with refreshments although she knew that Jane was more than able to handle a weekend of six guests. Moda and her husband, Remy, were expected to arrive at the same time, as well as Caleb and his new girlfriend, Peronia. They anticipated a weekend, like previous ones, of memories between good friends who had been apart for months and over a year. The weekend would be the new normal in a relaxed socially distanced world with masks, gloves, and sanitizers. Kascey had planned all the precautions, such as a safe way to have the dinner served, outdoor barbecues, and open terraces. Even Gradey's friend Ray would stay in the town and stop in for the barbecues and the beach parties, which would be outdoors. A weekend of calming times on the water's edge was upon them.

They drove through Massachusetts as they entered the cape and drove through the familiar town to Silent Manor. The welcoming feeling exuded by the structure of the building intensified as they drove closer. To Gradey's surprise, Caleb J Rolley's car was parked outside and had beat him to the celebrations.

"They are here already?" Gradey exclaimed as he customarily parked beside it as in college days.

"I know. I do not see Moda, though," Kascey said, inspecting their surroundings.

"They will be here soon. I am sure of it," he reassured her.

"I suppose," she replied nonchalantly and convinced. They disembarked and gathered their bags for the weekend. Caleb appeared on the porch to greet them as they walked in. He bore a striking image as he welcomed them in his usual fashion.

"Hello, hello. It looks like you have finally arrived," he said jokingly as the sweltering midday sun beamed.

"Yes, it is terrific that you are here and to finally see you," replied Gradey as they walked up the steps.

"Thanks. Let me introduce Peronia," he replied as he turned his commanding figure towards her. He presented a very petite and fit individual with sandy brown hair and smiling eyes. Caleb knew the authenticity of a college friend who would always be loyal. Having them meet Peronia, his serious partner, was important, and he knew that he was amongst close friends. Her family hailed from Romania, but she was raised in the Napa Valley and was incredibly devoted to her new-found love and relationship.

"Great to meet you," Gradey said. "We have heard so much about you. Welcome."

"Thank you for having me, and it is my pleasure," she replied in the sincerest way.

"Yes, you're very welcome, and same here. We have been looking forward to meeting you and hope that you will enjoy the weekend with us," said Kascey very succinctly.

"I am looking forward to it too. Caleb and I have been so excited to finally see you."

"I know. They are like brothers, and it has been a challenging time."

"Why don't we head in and put these down and then come back out here for the barbecue in a bit?" Gradey suggested.

"Perfect. Let me give you a hand with those bags," replied Caleb. He and Gradey had been college housemates and had been best friends ever since, having spent many weekends at the house.

Kascey and Gradey greeted Jane, who was busy in the kitchen. "Jane, it is delightful to see you again. How have you been?" Gradey asked.

"Wonderful, my son. I have been preparing all weekend for today, and I have not missed anything for the barbecue this afternoon. We have almost anything to grill: Vegetables, seafood, you name it," she replied proudly.

"Sounds delicious, and thank you for your time. It really smells good in here. Is that pecan and apple pie?" he asked.

"That's right. Now what would a holiday be without that?" she said proudly.

"Thank you," interjected Kascey. "We really appreciate your help. We can't wait to taste it."

Kascey and Gradey settled in the master bedroom this time and then strolled to the living room. She heard the engine of another car arrive and knew that it could only be Moda and Remy. She hastily ran out to greet them after such a lengthy period of time without seeing them.

"Hello," she welcomed them as they disembarked. "How was your ride down?"

"It was beautiful. We kept the top down," replied Moda as she emerged with round shades and a scarf to hold her hair. They had driven in from Staten Island and were ecstatic about the day out at the cape.

"That is good news, and so did we. Can you believe it? Remy, how are you? It is great to see you after so long," remarked Kascey.

"It is great to see you too, and it has been a long time. It was a beautiful ride, and it feels like things are almost back to normal."

"We brought some wine for the weekend." Moda offered a bag to Kascey.

"Thanks. That is so sweet. Look, have you met Caleb's new girlfriend?" she asked.

"Not yet," Moda said as she extended her hand to greet her.

"Nice to meet you," Peronia replied.

"Yes, and the same to you. We will get to know each other over the next few days," Moda said.

"We are so looking forward to it," she replied, impressed to have met someone so well known.

Remy acknowledged her with a nod of agreement. They carefully dragged their bags to the living room and headed to their seaside suite.

The time flew as Jane started to bring out the condiments and refreshments for the afternoon meal. Very experienced in her managing, she had been entertaining Gradey and his friends since junior high and was happy for this bit of nostalgia on Labor Day weekend. The afternoon tide had risen, and the surge of the waves brushed along the shoreline as the seagulls could be heard above. The breeze blew the tablecloth as Jane set the dishes upon the table.

Gradey awaited the arrival of one more person, and that was Ray, who was also a college friend. Again, he had spent many holidays with the family at Silent Manor and had attended their wedding over a year ago. Kascey had alternate plans and decided that it would be the perfect time for the ladies to bask in the open air before heading back to the hustle of the city.

"Ray, my friend. How long has it been?" asked Gradey. "It is good to see you. Thanks for coming."

"Great to see you too. It is my pleasure; I would not have missed it. It has been too long since I have been in Maine."

Ray was from Gradey's hometown and had known him all his life from junior high, although they became closer in college.

"Well we need an avid boater for our boat ride on Sunday with your skills. How has work been?" he asked.

"I am up for it," replied Ray. "Pretty Good. The markets are up again, as you know. So more hopeful moving forward."

"I know, and good to hear. Can I get you something?"

"Just something light; I have to drive back to town later, where I am staying."

"All right. It's coming right up," Gradey said.

"Caleb, has it been over a year?" he asked.

"Yes. It has been probably longer than that. I don't think that you have met Peronia."

"No. Incredibly pleased to meet you. I have known him a long time, so if you need any info, just let me know," he said remarkably.

"It is my pleasure too, and yes, I will," she said with a smile.

"How did you manage to meet her?" he said jokingly.

"With a lot of luck," answered Caleb placing his arm around her shoulder.

The small crowd settled on the grey wooden porch with a vast view of the ocean and talked about everything that mattered and was of consequence while reminiscing about old times. The sun began to set; it was getting late. They gathered sweaters and blankets to sit outside for the rest of the evening near the warm barbecue. Jane devotedly grilled the treats. The party continued until late in the evening, as they were so excited to see each other. The men got along like old friends as they casually opened bottles, ate their meal, and caught up on the past year.

The ladies made a point to become more acquainted with Peronia. Peronia was new to the group and laughed at old stories about occasions with Caleb and Gradey at the cape. She admitted that the lockdown had intensified their relationship and that she and Caleb had become inseparable. The friends chilled as the sun began to dip below the horizon. It was a relaxing evening and the perfect ending to an anticipated weekend that had been planned for months. They withstood the ocean's breeze as it grew cooler and their other halves later nestled next to them at the end of the evening. Moda and Remy retired while Remy drove back to the inn in town. Caleb and Gradey spent extra time to arrange their bags and equipment for the boat trip the following day.

"We should head out at about twelve; the water is predicted to be calm tomorrow."

"Yes. It should be a smooth sail around the harbour," replied Caleb.

"It should be. See you then," Gradey replied as they wrapped up the evening as the sun dipped below the horizon and the sky was a midnight blue. The words were etched in is mind, as he had been looking forward to the boat ride for weeks.

They gathered the blankets and glasses from the evening and took them inside before locking up. It was like the past weekends over the years, and it started to feel more like normal. It was past midnight, and there was another full day of excitement to look forward to. Kascey left the dishes to stack in the morning; she and Gradey were exhausted from a highly active day and fell into a deep slumber.

Kascey rose to Gradey gathering his belongings for the boat ride and the smell of brunch in the kitchen.

"Morning," she said, a little drained from the previous evening's celebrations.

"Morning," he replied as he looked around for his boat shoes.

"Are you heading out soon?" she asked.

"In about half an hour. I decided to let you sleep. It looked as if you really needed it," he replied.

"Thank you, dear. It smells delicious. What is she making?"

"Smells like blueberry pancakes and homemade oatmeal muffins," he replied.

"I really should get the recipe. I have been meaning to; I can smell banana purée."

"Yes. It is a sauce for the pancakes and maple syrup. Do you want anything?"

"No thanks. I will get there. I am hosting, remember?"

"Yes, I sure do," he replied.

"What do you think of Caleb's new girlfriend, Peronia?" she asked.

"She is fantastic. I am so happy for Caleb, and he is like

a changed man. I hope that it will all work out for him," he replied.

"Yes. I think that they are perfect together and that she really cares about him. It is all about him for her."

"Really? I am happy that he has found the right one."

They headed to the kitchen, where Jane was preparing the brunch.

"Good morning, you two. I hope that you had enough sleep. When I left, the party was still going."

"Yes, we had a late night, but we have rested well," replied Kascey.

"Yes, not to worry Jane. We are all well. This smells great."

"It is just a little brunch before your boat ride. We can make some fresh salads for those later for the beach."

"That is right, we are having a day at the beach. I am so looking forward to it."

The couples had brunch before Gradey and Caleb met Ray at the marina, where they stocked the boat for an afternoon on the ocean. The *Boston Whaler* was fully stocked as Grady steered the boat out of the marina and into the ocean.

Moda, Kascey, and Peronia gathered their beach gear and hats and found a perfect spot along the shore to camp out for the afternoon and picnic. They set up a few towels on the lounge chairs underneath the umbrella stand to shade them from the sun at high noon. They basked in the glow with wraps to protect their skin from the imposing rays, while they laughed and chatted about summer plans. It was a laid-back and hazy afternoon as Kascey took in the wide blue sky above her. She relished the various textures of her salad and the creamy homemade sauce.

The sun dipped more by 3.00 p.m., and the glow dimmed. They looked out at the horizon to see whether the men were in sight. The engine of the schooner could be heard as it drew closer to the bay, and they waved at them. Gradey, Ray, and Caleb spent more time on the boat and cruising along the perimeter before returning to the marina.

"What time do you think they will get back?" asked Peronia.

"Probably at about four. Usually they unstock and clean. It should not take long," replied Kascey understanding Peronia's longing for Caleb after hours apart. She had been the same way when she was out of the company of Gradey when they first met. She could not bear to be away from him for exceedingly long and counted the moments until he would return at similar gatherings.

"Yes, it should not be much longer," Moda reassured her, looking amused.

Kascey understood Peronia's willingness to get to know her, as she and Gradey were such a vital part of Caleb's life. Kascey found it unbearable watching from the sidelines, as she had experienced the same thing on weekends at Silent Manor when she did not want to leave his side during their early dating honeymoon phase. The ladies talked about their travels—especially Moda and Kascey, who had so many trips on which to reminisce.

The men had a view from the ocean towards the land. They could just decipher the figures on the beach. The sun dropped further towards the horizon as their day waned away. They reminisced about the good days at college and determined which was the best year.

"What do you think was the best year?"

"It was junior year," answered Caleb.

"Yes, I agree, we were almost there and not too serious," added Gradey.

"I enjoyed sophomore year," added Ray. "Life got too serious after that."

"I had to train abroad, and my senior year was filled with exams and applications," added Gradey.

"Well then, when was our best trip?" asked Caleb.

"Best trip was spring break sophomore year in Florida," Ray responded.

"I would have to say that it was the best trip," added Caleb.

"Really? What about freshman year Labor Day at the cape? Now *that* was a good holiday."

"You know, you are right," said Caleb. "That was a very good trip."

They took turns steering the boat back to the harbour and to the dock. Remy helped them to stock the Jeep with the equipment and bags before driving back to their partners. There was another barbecued dinner planned on the veranda overlooking on the beach.

"How was it? Did you see us waving to you from the shoreline?" Kascey asked Gradey as he entered the living room sun-baked and salted, with the cool air conditioning soothing his skin.

"Yes, we saw you. We waved back."

"Oh I missed that. It was too far away."

"I am just going to wash this salt off. I see Jane is almost done with the preparations for the grill."

"Yes. I had better see what is happening with that," she replied dutifully.

"I am sure that she can manage it. So what did you all get up to?" he asked.

"Nothing much. Just an enjoyable day at the beach. And I am sure that Peronia is happy now. I think that she was pining for Caleb," she commented.

"I see. They are close."

"Yes. I remember those days and can really empathize," she replied.

"You do?" He smirked as he selected his outfit for the evening.

"This has been such a perfect weekend. I have not been stressed about work, and you have been so much calmer. This has really done us some good."

"Yes. It is just what we needed. We have finally been able to socialize and to see my crew again." It had been exceptionally long since he had murmured those words—probably since college.

"I know; it has been so thrilling watch you all interact again. I am glad that we planned this. We should try it again at the end of the summer."

"We definitely should."

They casually strolled outside, where Jane was setting up the buffet. "You have outdone yourself," Gradey remarked.

"Really? Just a repeat of last night. It is easy, and besides, I would prefer to do this for you all. You are still so much like family."

"Thank you, and you are like our family too," he replied.

"Yes, it all looks great," Kascey replied. "Let me know if there is anything that I can do to help," She was aware that there would be more holidays and happy memories to come. To her it was a fresh start with the same company.

They met the group on the veranda and once again enjoyed an evening of camaraderie. This time there was a firework display across the cape and the smell of the barbecue and baked pies brought nostalgic memories of past holidays at Silent Manor. The manor was quiet and held the memories of the legacy of the family that lived within the walls. They had surfaced from a challenging year. It would see more celebrations, parties, birthdays, and marriages as the changing seasons of life occurred. The foundation remained, and the stability of the people remained. It was the centre of the past and would hold the future of the family, filled with treasures from holidays and vacations past. Along the coast of the shore, there sat a holiday cottage set further inland behind the swaying sea oats and beach ferns that held the laughter and the companionship of those who entered, and it was called Silent Manor.